DENVER
STRIKE

DENVER STRIKE

RANDY WAYNE
WHITE
WRITING AS CARL RAMM

OPEN ROAD
INTEGRATED MEDIA
NEW YORK

Cover design by Andy Ross

ISBN: 978-1-5040-3523-1

This edition published in 2016 by Open Road Integrated Media, Inc.
180 Maiden Lane
New York, NY 10038
www.openroadmedia.com

DENVER
STRIKE

ONE

James Hawker knew at a glance that the woman and her two kids were in trouble.

The three of them had been brought to this remote valley of grass and wild flowers high above Denver in the Colorado Rockies. They had been housed in the old herder's cabin by the cold trout stream that rushed through the aspens, out of the snowy peaks.

They had been told to live quietly in the cabin, to stay away from civilization until their "problem" had been resolved.

Hawker was familiar with the woman's problem: there were men who would happily torture or kill her and her children to get what they wanted from the woman's father.

Hawker also knew that the only way to resolve her problem was to eliminate those men.

Now, Hawker decided, was the time to do some eliminating.

He reached into his canvas duffel and withdrew a black alloy bow attached to an abbreviated rifle stock.

It was a Cobra crossbow, military issue. The crossbow had

a killing range of nearly a half-mile, and it could send its dart-size arrows traveling through the heart of a man at a speed of a hundred yards per second. Each dart was specially made so it could be fitted with tiny weights to compensate for distance or windage. The bow itself had a 4×–7× zoom scope with a built-in self-illuminating compass.

As Hawker picked up the bow, he wondered what the Arapaho warriors who had hunted in these mountains three hundred years ago would have thought of this strange dark-red-haired man in his camouflage jump suit and black wool watch cap, holding this strangest of all bows.

They would have probably thought he was some kind of weird mountain god.

In a way, they would have been right.

Today, anyway, he was playing God. Today he would save a few lives and he would take a few lives.

It was a role he had played many times before, all across America.

Hawker used the self-cocking lever to break the bow almost double, like an air rifle. The bow locked back into place, and he fitted one of the arrows—bolts—onto the shooting track. After checking to make sure the safety pin was on, he rested his eye against the scope and used his left hand to dial to its lowest power.

The scope melted the two hundred yards between the cabin and his position on the mountainside into almost nothing. He could see the heavy logs of the cabin mortised by gray wattle, the planking of the slanted roof, smoke drifting out of the raw stone chimney, the Appaloosa mare grazing among the sheep on the hillside, and the wide door on its rusted hinges as it opened out onto the dirt path that led past the split-timber fence to the river.

He could see, too, the woman, with a towel in her hand, walking toward the river where the aspens and the willows met in a screen of yellow and white leaves, could see her using her fingers to brush her buttock-length black hair.

Hawker swung the scope back toward the cabin. Where were the two kids? There they were, two sets of big dark eyes at the window: K.D., the nine-year-old boy, and Dolores, the lovely, fawnlike seven-year-old girl.

When the vigilante was sure the children were all right, he focused the scope on the back of the woman as she swayed toward the river.

The woman's name was Lomela. Hawker guessed her to be in her early thirties; though she looked younger, she might have been older. Lomela was the illegitimate daughter of old Robert Charles Carthay, the silver prospector, and his Hispanic/Indian bunkmate, housekeeper, and (when he was mining the high basins for silver) pack mule. Lomela had the short, stout body of a Mexican and the long legs and Apache-face of an Indian. Her hair was glossy blue-black, as healthy as an animal pelt, and her eyes were a shy brown.

Hawker had never met Lomela or her two children. But he had spent the last eight hours on this mountainside watching over them.

Now he watched her closely.

Lomela knelt at the clear river and dipped her hands in, drinking. Then, with the abrupt this-way-that-way look of a deer, the woman stood and stretched herself. Crossing her hands in front of her, she stripped off her white blouse, then stepped out of her boots and jeans.

Now she wore only sheer beige panties. Hawker watched her through the scope as she threw her hair back over her shoulder and held her arms out as if to embrace the sun. Her body was more attractive than Hawker would have guessed. He would have expected her to be brown and doughy and shapeless. She was none of those things.

Her shoulders became narrower without the baggy blouse, and her chest expanded and took shape. Childbirth had flattened her heavy breasts, but the nipples, tiny on the vast dollar-size brown circles of areolas, still pointed upward. When she leaned over the river to drink again, Hawker could see the washboard steps of her ribs beneath the swinging breasts, and he could see the meaty expansion of hips and thighs beneath her panties.

Now she stripped off the panties, scratched at her pubic hair with the unconscious ease of a wild creature, and then ran into the cold water of the river.

It was bath time in the high country of the autumn Rockies.

Lomela's little boy and girl poked their heads out the door to watch.

Hawker knew that they were not the only ones who were watching.

He twisted the eyepiece of the zoom scope to full power. He began a methodical search of the dense brush below him. Finally, he saw it again: the wide fingers of a man's hand, the ugly snout of a sawed-off shotgun. This time, though, he also saw a chunk of the man's head as he leaned eagerly forward from his blind so that he might better see the naked woman.

How many more of them were there?

The vigilante had seen only this man for certain. But he had seen a glimmer of metal or glass on the hill behind the cabin, and he had seen crows flush from the aspen grove to his right, so he suspected there were more of them.

They had come into the basin more than two hours ago, and Hawker had awaited their first move.

But they seemed content to lie low until dark to strike—a sign of patience that distressed Hawker, for it showed the men to be competent, professional, and very, very dangerous.

Hawker knew he wouldn't have much of a chance against them after the sun dropped behind the mountain.

He had to sniff them out now, take them one by one, and hope to Christ he got them all.

Below, the woman was climbing out of the river, her hair hanging in a wet rope down her back, her hips swinging, her breasts bouncing, her whole body glowing with the cold. She found the towel beneath her clothes and buffed herself dry.

From the door of the cabin, the boy and girl stepped out—only to be waved back inside by their naked mother. With the sure intuition of a woman, she seemed to know there was danger nearby, and she wasn't going to let her children take any chances.

As Hawker looked at the woman, he thought about the bizarre circumstances and the strange chain of events that had brought him to these mountains. The story Jacob Montgomery Hayes had told him involved a mixture of piracy, international finance, and Old West claim-jumping. And the whole story revolved around this woman who now stood naked before him.

I've watched her move all around today, Hawker thought, and she never once struck me as being physically desirable—until now. With her clothes off, she has the sloe-eyed, big-breasted, spread-thighed broodmare look, the look of a woman who lives to be bedded and bear young . . .

Hawker shook the image from his mind. Voyeurism is bad enough, he thought. Combined with adolescent fantasies, it makes you into a singularly unattractive middle-aged man.

Once again, one of the children—the boy—poked his head through the door. This time, Hawker stiffened as he saw the man on the ledge beneath him stand, balance himself, then exchange the shotgun for a long-barreled rifle. Hawker recognized the rifle. It was a Remington model 700, the Mauseractioned weapon that, in its military version, had been used as a highly effective sniper rifle.

The man now lifted the rifle toward the head of the child who stood in the distant doorway.

Why would the man have waited so long only to fire now? It didn't make sense.

But Hawker didn't take time to ponder. He got noiselessly to his feet, brought the cross hairs of the Cobra to bear on the back of the man's neck, saw the reflexive stiffening of the man just before the Remington exploded, then squeezed the trigger of the crossbow.

The arrow was a momentary sliver of light between two snowy peaks, Hawker saw it flash once, then disappear into the pale hush of the aspens. The Remington made no sound.

Now it was an entirely different scene through the zoom scope. The vigilante could see that the man lay face downward while his hands clawed at the bright arrow in his neck. His feet made a random, thumping motion as they hammered at the earth. Blood splotched the pale weeds.

Beyond, the woman had thrown her clothes over her shoulder and now walked unconcerned toward the snug little cabin. She had obviously heard nothing.

Hawker was relieved. If she had not heard, the men had not heard either.

The vigilante loaded another bolt into the crossbow and began to move toward the expanse of trees where he had seen crows flush.

TWO

The snowy peaks glittered with the cold light of dusk as Hawker began to hunt along the mountainside.

Back in Florida, back in the mangrove, mosquito, and tarpon country where he had been when Hayes had wired him, it was September. But September in Florida had absolutely nothing in common with September in the Colorado Rockies.

September in Florida was desert-calm mornings on the sea, suffocating afternoons beneath a sun the size of a full moon, and still-humid nights dank with the protein odor of mud flats as hot as human viscera.

In the Colorado Rockies, though, September was a month of transition. It was a clutch month that shifted directly into autumn. Here the aspens were turning silver on the high mountain peaks. The air was as startlingly cool as skin bracer. Ski resorts were already preparing their lift gear. The mountains seemed to hush a little with the expectation of snow.

James Hawker took a deep gulp of the thin, cold air. Breathing was the biggest difference, though—*trying* to breathe.

Climbing over the rugged hillside, the vigilante forced himself to move slowly, to take it easy. True, the sun was floating toward the mountain's crest; nightfall was coming fast. But he still had to take his time. In this oxygen-poor air, hurrying would leave his lungs burning, his legs shaking.

He had to move slowly, deliberately, if he were to succeed.

Hawker dropped down off a rock ledge and landed by the corpse of the man he had just shot. The man lay on his stomach, his hands frozen around the nub of aluminum arrow that protruded through his neck. The vigilante used his foot to roll the man over: long, hippie-length black hair, a bluish beard, a meaty, acne-scarred face, khaki pants, hunting boots, a Smith & Wesson .38 strapped to his hips, a red nylon satchel filled with ammunition for the Remington 700 and for the sawed-off shotgun that lay beside him in the grass.

The vigilante used his hands to search for identification, but he found none.

He did find, however, a pocket-size UHF transceiver in the man's jacket. Hawker took the radio and touched the transmitter button twice, hoping the static would bring some reply.

It did.

"Come back, red team. Is that you? Still waiting for your sound, red team, still waiting for your sound. Is game still in sight?"

The sound the speaker was waiting for was, of course, a rifle shot.

Hawker held the radio far from his lips. "Still waiting for clear view," Hawker said. "Standing by."

The man with the other radio had spoken just enough for

the vigilante to use the antenna as a direction finder and get the general direction of the speaker's whereabouts.

He was the one who had frightened the crows nearby.

Hawker pulled the arrow from the man's neck, wiped the razor-sharp killing blade in the grass, then stuck the radio in his pocket.

He began to work his way slowly along the ridge, stopping occasionally to survey the trees ahead. Twice the radio squawked, startling him, so he finally turned it off.

When he judged that he was very near the second man, though, he halted in the brush and switched the radio back on. He touched the mike key twice, spun the volume down, and listened.

He could hear nothing from the radio, but he could hear the faint voice of a man talking nearby.

Hawker raised the scope of the Cobra crossbow to his right eye and looked.

Hidden in a pouch formed by rocks and a fallen pine were two men. They were out of the same mold as the man he had just shot: long, greasy hair, hunting clothes, shotguns at their sides, handguns in holsters. Hawker had never met them, yet he knew their type all too well. These were the modern guns-for-hire. You found them among the vicious motorcycle gangs or in the drug-trafficking or porno rings. They were sadists, and they loved their work. A high percentage of them were drug addicts, and they would do absolutely anything to make money so they could support their habits. If killing a woman and her two children paid big, then they would do it without the blink of an eye.

The vigilante lowered the crossbow, wondering just how he should go about it. How could he eliminate both of these men without making noise? There was at least one more man—but probably more—on the other side of the valley. Hawker had seen the glitter of metal earlier. If he used the Colt Commando assault rifle that he carried across his back in a sling, the noise would frighten off the rest of his quarry. And he wanted them all. He didn't want any to escape.

But if he used the crossbow, one of the men would certainly have time to cry out or to get off a couple of shots with the Winchester model 12s they carried.

Hawker decided to take a closer look.

Leaning into the mountain, he moved down the hill sideways, his hands gaining purchase from bushes, taking great care not to start any small rock-slides that would give his position away.

When he was within forty yards of the men, he stopped. The biggest advantage Hawker had was the fact that the men he was hunting had absolutely no idea that they were being hunted.

That gave him an idea. No longer trying to be silent, Hawker got to his feet and walked innocently toward their hiding place. He actually began to whistle. For all the men knew, he was a tourist lost in the mountain wilderness.

Hawker kept the Cobra at his side in his right hand, cocked and ready—just as he held the Colt Commando, safety off, in his left hand. When he got close enough to see the men, he smiled mildly and, still walking toward them, said, "Hey, you guys don't know where I can find a phone booth, do you?"

Hawker expected at least a moment of uncertainty from the two men. They were startled all right—but there was nothing uncertain about them. They knew exactly what they wanted to do. Hawker saw them both lift their weapons at the same time, but he never gave them a chance to fire. He had no alternative. He raised the Cobra, fired too quickly, and the aluminum shaft buried itself in the side of the man closest to him.

The man gave a horrible scream that echoed through the mountains. But his scream was not nearly as loud as the quick burst from the Colt Commando assault rifle that Hawker used to kill the second man.

The report of the automatic weapon seemed to echo forever through the hills.

Damn it! Hawker snarled beneath his breath as he stooped over the corpses of the two men. He could practically hear the men on the other side of the valley scrambling to safety. He went through the pockets, finding cigarettes, candy bars, matches, money, and a Glad-Wrap bag full of marijuana, but no identification of any kind.

Hawker tried to get the arrow from between the ribs of the man he had shot with the Cobra. But the arrow had disappeared inside his chest cavity—another reason for Hawker to be angry at himself.

He had bungled the job—thought too slowly and shot too quickly.

Blame it on the high altitude, he thought. Your brain isn't getting enough air.

What brain, dumb shit? he railed at himself.

Hawker picked up the second radio and touched the mike key. "All teams come in; come in all teams."

Silence. If the man or men on the other side of the valley had a radio, they weren't about to answer.

Hawker stood and looked at the cabin. He could see the woman, now clothed, standing in the doorway staring in his direction. There was a look of fear and confusion on her face. What had made the terrible sounds she had just heard?

Hawker began to make his way quickly down the hillside—but then a terrible thought entered his mind. The orders of the first man he had killed had been to shoot one—or maybe both—of the children.

Maybe the man or men on the other side of the valley had been ordered to shoot the woman.

The vigilante sprang onto a great wedge of rock. "Lomela!" he yelled. "Get inside!"

The mountains threw his voice back at him over and over again.

The woman looked up, startled. She touched her hand to her forehead, straining to see.

"Lomela, get inside the cabin!"

Shaking her head, the woman stepped back just as the entire door seal was blown off by some heavy-caliber weapon. She had so narrowly escaped being hit that Hawker stood frozen for a moment—but then rocks near his feet exploded as the rifleman turned his weapon toward Hawker.

The vigilante jumped to the ground, rolled, and zigzagged into the brush. Twice more, the rifleman shot at Hawker, once severing a branch from over his head. But the vigilante continued to make his way around the rim of the valley toward the place where the rifleman must be hidden. The sun was behind the western snowy peaks now, and a frigid wind blew down from the ice capped heights.

It was ridiculous to look for a lone man in these thousands of acres of woods, but the vigilante ex-cop continued. There was a chance—however slim. And he had to take it.

Finally, he was near. He knew he must be near. He could see the eastern side of the cabin now, could see that the woman was too frightened or too smart to show any lights inside. He pictured her and the two children huddled in a corner beneath a blanket, the way pioneer women had waited in terror for Indians so many generations before.

Hawker stopped on the mountainside, waiting. Below him, the valley, the river, the wild flowers, and the log cabin became a fantasy world of rich light as the sun set—then ever-weakening light until the sun was gone, leaving the valley in a cold and lonesome afterglow.

From his canvas backpack he took a pair of Steiner military binoculars and searched the hillside. The Steiners were the best nonpowered night vision glasses in the world. The wide lenses sucked in all available light, highlighted detail, and transformed grays to whites so that looking through them at dusk was like looking through normal glasses at midday.

Hawker saw the man then: a lone figure standing against an aspen tree, his rifle resting on a low branch as he aimed toward the cabin in the distance.

Obviously, the man was waiting for one last shot, hoping,

perhaps, that the woman would light a lamp and cross before a window.

But now it was Hawker who had the last shot. Quickly, he put the Steiners away and raised the Cobra crossbow—but he didn't fire. Through the binoculars, the man had been clearly visible. Now, looking through the narrow hunting scope, he couldn't find the man, who was invisible in the gloomy dusk.

Damn, Hawker whispered.

He would have to get closer if he wanted a shot. Much closer.

The vigilante slipped the backpack over his shoulder, adjusted the Colt Commando, then set off slowly down the mountainside. The temperature had fallen with the sun. His hands felt clumsy in the cold, and his breath fogged before him. Every few dozen yards he would stop and look through the Steiners again to make sure the gunman had not moved.

The gunman stood immobile, confident that he could not be seen.

Finally, when Hawker was sure he was close enough, he stopped behind a great tall pine and put the backpack and the crossbow on the ground. He took up the binoculars in his left hand and steadied the assault rifle in the other. The Colt Commando could fire its twenty-round clip in the blink of an eye—eight hundred rounds per minute, if you could feed it fast enough. All Hawker had to do was get a rough sighting through the binoculars, then spray the darkness with the Commando. The gunman would not survive.

Hawker peered through the Steiners, ready to fire—but the assassin was gone. The vigilante swept the glasses back and forth, hoping he had searched the wrong tree or the wrong ledge.

No, the gunman had definitely left.

Shaking his head in disgust, Hawker reached to retrieve his backpack—then threw up an arm against the dark shape that was descending upon him.

The man had been waiting for him, waiting in the shadows on a head-high ledge, and he jumped on Hawker with a jarring impact, driving him to the ground. Then they were rolling, the two of them tumbling down the mountainside in the darkness, fighting for their lives.

The man had a knife, a dark-bladed hunting knife, in his left hand. The vigilante got his own hands up in time and locked them around his attacker's wrist, unable to do anything but hold the knife inches away from his face as they rolled down through brush, over rocks. Then there was another terrible impact, and the vigilante was floating free; then he landed with a *whoof* on the other side of the shallow precipice that the two of them had hit.

Hawker got painfully to his feet just in time to duck the savage kick that the assassin threw at his head. The vigilante timed the next kick and caught the man's leg in midflight, twisting and lifting at the same time. The assassin gave a little squeal of fear as he flew through the air, landed, and rolled upright. Hawker went after him immediately. In the darkness, the man's face seemed grotesquely wide; it made a skin-slap sound as Hawker drove his right fist into it again and again.

The man swung a looping left hand at Hawker's stomach,

swung so slowly that Hawker almost didn't bother to move—but then he felt a deep electric pain explode in his left arm: the man still had the knife!

Hawker ripped the knife free, kicked the man savagely in the stomach, then drove the knife deep into his back as he buckled over. The man threw himself grotesquely onto the ground, clawing at his own back. Within a few moments, he moved no more.

Hawker stood, bent at the waist, hands on his knees, fighting to get his breath. It seemed impossible to breathe in these mountains. How could anyone live up here!

Then he walked wearily back up the hill and found his backpack and the assault rifle. From the backpack he took his tiny Tonka flashlight, twisted the cap, and inspected his left arm. The camouflage material of his jump suit was blood-soaked. He ripped the material away and saw that the knife had only gouged a chunk of meat from the underside of his arm. It didn't seem like a serious wound, but he was bleeding steadily, and Hawker knew he needed help.

He took a handkerchief from his pack and wrapped it snugly around his arm. Then he remembered he had left the knife in the back of the man below—the knife with his fingerprints all over it. With a growling sigh of disgust, he backtracked, yanked the man's knife free, and carried it halfway down the mountain with him before he wiped the steel clean and hid it under a rock.

At the edge of the clearing, fifty yards from the cabin, he stopped. The woman had still lighted no lamps, and Hawker felt a pang of sympathy for the frightened woman and her two children. For all they knew, death was waiting right outside their door.

"Lomela! My name is James Hawker. Can you hear me? A policeman friend of yours in Denver sent me—Tom Dulles. I'm here to help!"

Hawker listened to his own echo fade into silence. A great cold moon was lifting over the snowy peaks now, casting a milky light over the gurgling river and the still fields. Hawker felt the beauty of it like a pain deep inside him, and he realized he must be giddy with shock, maybe even in danger of blacking out. He had to hurry; he needed the woman.

"Lomela! I met your father! I met Robert Carthay, and he told me about the silver mine. You have nothing to fear now. The men who were after you are gone."

A warm light bloomed in the cabin windows, but now Hawker seemed unable to walk. He felt dizzy; he felt nauseous; his legs seemed unable or unwilling to move away from the beauty of the mountain valley frozen in moonlight. If he could only sit for a while, rest for just a bit, then he could travel.

Hawker leaned toward the ground, and the ground rushed up to meet him. He hit with a thud, then all was cold and fuzzy as a rapid darkness took his brain.

THREE

Hawker was aware of a great radiant warmth moving through him, a wonderful feeling of heat that embraced his entire body.

Then he was sitting bolt upright, staring into the flames of a hearth fire. He lay in front of the fire with a goose-down comforter over him. The woman stood peering at him, fire-shadows flickering across her brown face.

He lay on the plank floor of the cabin. There were deer-skins over the windows, and a kerosene lamp cast a yellow circle of light, showing a wood stove, cane-backed chairs, a hand pump, stacked dishes, and a door that opened into a darkened room.

Hawker felt a dull ache in his left arm, and he remembered the fight he had had with the man with the knife. He used his right hand to rub his bleary eyes. "How long have I been unconscious?"

The woman stared at him, unmoving. There was a blanket across her lap, and her hands were beneath the blanket. "An hour. Maybe longer. You were delirious off and on; you came and went. How do you feel now?" Her voice was too high, too countrified to fit the no-nonsense, almost handsome quality of her face. It was like hearing Ingrid Bergman speak with Minnie Pearl's voice.

"I feel like I've been hit over the head with a sledge," Hawker said, straightening himself. The blanket slid down over his chest, and he saw that his arm had been neatly bandaged and that he wore only his underwear. "Did you get me in here all by yourself?"

"You helped some. You half-walked, half-crawled. You lost a lot of blood. What happened? Did you get shot?"

"Stabbed. There were four men in the hills. I—chased them away. The fourth man got me with his knife."

"Do you really mean you chased them away? Or did you kill them?" The woman's dark eyes were totally without emotion or mercy as she asked the question.

Hawker said slowly, "I killed them. All of them. That's what they wanted to do to you, isn't it? You or your kids—it didn't matter to them. Just as long as they had at least one of you alive to use as a bargaining tool."

"They'd do anything for my daddy's silver mine, wouldn't they? They'd kill, kidnap, lie—anything."

Hawker nodded. "That's right. And don't forget it."

The woman let the blanket slide off her lap so that now the vigilante could see the long-barreled revolver she held tightly in both hands. It had been aimed at him the entire time. "Not much chance of me forgetting it, Mr. Whatever-your-name-is," she said coldly. "Those men were shooting down here without a care in the world at my two babies, who haven't done a lick of harm to any creature on this earth. Men as mean as that don't deserve a trial nor words. All they deserve is a bullet in the head. Now you tell me right now why I shouldn't put a bullet through your head."

"Because I'm not one of them, Lomela," Hawker said calmly. "I was sent here to help you. I already told you that. Tom Dulles sent me. Isn't Tom a friend of yours? He was worried about you. He knows how badly Bill Nek wants your father's mine. He knows Bill Nek will stop at nothing."

The woman seemed unconvinced. "You could have got Tom's name anyplace. You could be making the whole thing up. It's not like I can get on the telephone and give Tom a call. The nearest phone in these parts is thirty miles over rough country."

"I know that you and Tom were lovers, Lomela. I know that he was in love with you before his wife recovered and made it—implausible—for you and him to continue as man and woman. He told me how badly he felt about it all."

The woman was silent for a long moment of appraisal before she finally said, "He purely did feel bad; both of us did." There was a touching, faraway quality to her voice as she continued. "His wife had those brain operations, and then she was in the coma for more than a year, and you couldn't hardly call him still married. There didn't seem to be nothing at all wrong in Tom and me finding each other and falling in love. He took good care of his wife, and I took good care of him. He was a wanting, needing man, filled with loneliness and hurt. But he also knew what was right and what was wrong. And when his wife woke up one day, he knew we couldn't go on."

"He still cares about you," Hawker said gently. "That's why he sent me."

The woman stood and placed the revolver on the mantelpiece above the fire. She stooped and fitted another log onto the grate. Her baggy cotton blouse was tucked into her jeans, and Hawker could see her heavy breasts silhouetted against the fire. "I know he still cares. But it's not like the old way we cared for each other. Now we're more like kinfolk who are friendly to each other, that kind of caring." The woman turned and looked at Hawker. "I believe Tom sent you. And I surely do thank you for killing those men. Are you going to get in a lot of trouble for it? Or are you a policeman?"

The vigilante almost smiled at the girlish naïveté of her question—as if a cop or anyone else could kill four men without almost certainly getting into some kind of trouble. "I'm not a policeman," Hawker said. "And, come morning, I'll make sure the bodies of the men aren't found. Unless you talk, there's not too much chance of my getting into trouble."

The woman nodded, satisfied. "Good," she said. "I kind of knew someone was up here. I felt it all day. I don't know how I knew, but I did."

"I was the only one up here all day. The other men got there about two hours before you heard the shots."

"You watched me and my babies all day long without saying a word?" The woman raised her eyebrows, impressed. But then she realized something. "So you was up there when I took my afternoon bath?"

Hawker nodded. "I watched you through binoculars"—he smiled—"and a very nice bath it was, too. You had quite an

24

audience. The men were there then, too. Actually, you helped draw them out. When you started taking your clothes off, they came out of hiding."

The woman nodded with emphasis. "Good. Then it was worth running around stark naked in front of a bunch of strange men. I'd do it again if I thought it would help keep my babies safe."

"Where are your children, anyway?"

The woman motioned toward the darkened room. "In there, asleep. They purely have had some time of it, dodging bullets and worrying about being attacked. There was a time when I used to think that getting divorced from their daddy was the worst thing that could happen to them. I didn't know how wrong I was."

"Things get a lot more complicated when you're rich," Hawker said.

The woman only shrugged as she poured tea from a kettle into a mug. She handed the cup to him, then took a seat beside him on the rug. "I just hope we all live long enough to get a chance to enjoy it," she said without bitterness. "It's a long story; a hard one to understand."

"I've already heard the story," said James Hawker. "And I already understand."

What Hawker understood was that, by rights, Lomela and her family should have already been enjoying great wealth for many years. God knows, her father, Robert Charles Carthay, and his partners had worked hard enough. Yet only one of them ever prospered.

Sitting in the plush lounge of the Slope Hotel in Denver, Carthay had told Hawker all about it.

It had all begun more than fifty years ago, in Denver, when four young men had decided to live out the alluring dream: to strike it rich as silver prospectors. Carthay was the thinker among them, the born leader. Jimmy Estes was the sprite, the camp clown. Chuck Phillips was darkly handsome and mercurial. Bill Nek could be moody, brooding, brilliant, or hilarious, depending on his mood.

For the first years, just the excitement of their rough-and-ready lives was enough for these men. They had the mountains, fresh air, good food, and an occasional bottle of whiskey, and they had their friendship. It was a very close friendship, for the four men had signed an agreement—a covenant—to share all finds, whether discovered individually or together. But they found little silver to speak of, just enough to stake them again to more months in the Colorado wilderness.

But then Jimmy Estes did make a find. He struck a moderately rich vein of silver within spitting distance of the old railroad tracks that filed through Gore Range, high in the Rockies.

The four men celebrated. They went to Denver, where they drank, they ate, they had women—and the first man up and in the claim office the next day was Bill Nek, the brooding one, and he took it all for himself.

Over the years, Nek parlayed that stolen vein into one of the greatest mining fortunes in Colorado. He became known regionally as the Silver King—tarnished silver, some said, because his methods of acquisition were often brutal and illegal, though always carefully concealed by a masterly and expensive use of the law.

Conversely, Robert Charles Carthay, Jimmy Estes, and Chuck Phillips remained poor prospecting desert rats, making just enough money to get by on. As the years went by and they kept up their fruitless prospecting, the local stories about them became wilder and wilder. To Colorado's New Guard (moneyed Easterners who contrived Western accents and wore cowboy hats in Vail's plush watering holes), the three old men became comic figures, legendary buffoons who represented the shaky social makeup of most old-time Coloradoans. "Loony" was the most charitable description.

Jimmy Estes and Chuck Phillips never married; Robert Carthay took a Hispanic and Indian mixed-breed as his long-term companion. The woman who now sat beside Hawker by the fire was the attractive result.

The story could have ended right there—one more tragic tale of prospecting in the West. But it didn't end there because Carthay, Estes, and Phillips never gave up their search for silver. Finally, three years ago—more than fifty years after the four partners had signed the covenant—they found it. They found what they had always dreamed of finding but had never really expected to find at all: a vein of silver so wide, so rich, that it was far beyond any of their wildest expectations. As safely and as secretively as a combined 150 years of prospecting experience allowed, they registered their find, calling the mine the Chiquita, in memory of Carthay's eldest daughter, who'd died tragically when she was only ten. They had commenced mining operations, gradually extending and building a mine. Yet before they had realized any profit, Bill Nek, the Silver King, arrived on the scene demanding that they sell him the mine.

He was wasting his time, of course. The mine wasn't for sale, not for any price, and certainly not to him. But Nek was a rich man, not used to taking no for an answer. He began to apply pressure, trying to grind the old men down. But Carthay and Estes and Phillips hadn't survived for fifty years in the mountains by being soft. They told Nek to go to hell more than once—and maybe once too often: the three of them were kidnapped.

Nek had his hired guns take them to an abandoned mine in the high mountains. There they were kept. Nek couldn't simply have them killed because their joint will would transfer ownership of the silver mine to Lomela through a complex trust that made the mine virtually untouchable. So the Silver King had the infuriating task of keeping his three old partners alive while breaking them to the point where they would sell the mine to him. The old men were tortured, but never beyond the point of endurance, for Nek couldn't take the chance of killing any one of them.

Finally, Robert Carthay escaped. He found Lomela and warned her; she told Tom Dulles, a Denver cop and her former lover. It was clear that Nek would stop at nothing to get Carthay back and make him sign over the papers. And Nek had the money and the hired gunmen to do it.

Dulles realized that it was an extraordinary situation—and that it called for extraordinary measures.

Like most of the cops in major cities around America, he had heard rumors of a lone auburn-haired stranger who feared nothing for he no longer had anything to lose.

Dulles sent Lomela and her father to separate hiding

places, then turned his attention to getting in touch with the world's deadliest vigilante.

Hawker was impossible to find. But by now he had such a complex network of sympathizers around the nation that it was just as impossible for people in need to remain beyond his hearing.

The vigilante heard about Carthay and his plight. He was on a plane out of Miami the next day, bound for the Mile High City.

"That's the story your father told me two days ago in Denver," Hawker said, finishing the mug of tea. "Tom Dulles brought him in to talk to me. It was a short meeting. Your father wore a big Western hat and glasses, a kind of disguise so he wouldn't be recognized. Apparently Nek has spies every-where. Money buys even the most unlikely spies. Dulles told me where your father was being hidden and where you were hiding. I decided that Nek was most likely to send his goons after you. If he got you and maybe killed one of your children, then he would have plenty of blackmail leverage on your father and his two partners."

The woman laughed softly. "You know what the really strange thing is? All those years after Bill Nek double-crossed him, my daddy still wouldn't say anything bad about that man. My daddy was fierce loyal, and he just couldn't bring himself to say anything bad about a man who had been a partner of his."

"Come to think of it," said Hawker, "he didn't have much bad to say about Nek two days ago when I met him."

"It's not because Daddy likes Nek. Don't think for a moment that's the reason. He thinks Bill Nek is the lowest creature on earth. He double-crossed his partners way back when Jimmy Estes found that first vein of silver, and he's spent his whole life double-crossing people. Daddy used to just sort of shake his head when folks would tell him that Nek was stealing, cheating—even killing—to get what he wanted. I really don't think Daddy believed the stories. But he believes them now."

Hawker put his empty mug on the floor and settled back, looking into the fire. Outside, the wind had freshened. It moaned through the high peaks and rattled the windows. Hawker pulled the goose-down quilt up over his chest. "I'm glad you came and helped me," he said. "I would have frozen to death out there."

"Don't talk anymore," Lomela said. "I'll get some warm soup in you come morning. We need to build your strength back up. You'll still be feverish for a while, so you best sleep here by the fire. If you need anything, just call out. I'm a light sleeper. I'll hear you."

The vigilante let his head sink deeper into the pillow as he stared into the fire.

Soon, he was asleep.

FOUR

He awoke with his teeth chattering, sweat beading on his forehead, trembling uncontrollably.

The fire was now just a mound of glowing embers. The cabin shifted in the wind, its timbers creaking. The moon had disappeared, leaving a silver halo above the snowy peaks to the west. Hawker knew it was very late.

He threw back the blanket and found the wood-box. The plank floor was like ice beneath his feet. He knelt before the fire and fitted two sections of splintered wood into the coals before his back turned to water and his lungs began to labor in the thin air. He tried to catch himself, but couldn't in time. He sprawled across the floor with a *whoof*.

Then Lomela was beside him, clucking and cooing, scolding him for being up. She cradled his head in her lap and rubbed his hands briskly, trying to warm him. She wore a granny nightgown of brushed cotton, and Hawker pressed against her, colder than he had ever been.

"You purely do have a fever. How long have you been shaking like this?"

"I-I-I don-don-don't know."

She pulled him back to the rug, hugged her body close to his, then dragged the blanket over the two of them. "Here, this ought to warm you. No, don't say anything. Just go to sleep. That's what I'm fixing to do."

Hawker awoke later. He didn't know how much later. He was no longer shivering, but that was not the reason he had awakened. The woman was still beside him, her comfortable body fitted against his. Her leg was thrown over his thigh, and he was aware of a gentle warm pressure against his right knee. The woman's left hand was moving in a circular motion over his bare back, while her right hand nuzzled the hair on his abdomen. There had been a subtle change in her body tone, some deep, primal change of which Hawker was aware on an animal level.

He stirred against her, lifted one hand, and brushed the hot weight of her breast accidentally.

Lomela's moan was like a sob.

He felt the gentle pressure against his knee increase, a pressure that grew hotter and damper with each second. Hawker touched his palm to the woman's slowly writhing buttocks, sliding along the soft curvature of her waist and ribs. He wrapped her hair in his fist and pulled her face to his, surprised at the eagerness of her lips, the hunger of her tongue.

"I've been so long without a man," she whispered in long exhalation. "Don't know what came over me. Being near you felt so good. But it ain't fair, you being sick—"

"I'm feeling better," Hawker whispered back. "See?"

Lomela's laughter was more a feral growl. "You purely do *feel* healthy. Real healthy. I may feel a fool come morning, but right now I just don't care. A woman shouldn't have to go so long without having a man. Being without a man weakens a woman's body, and it makes her soul go all hungry. That's how I feel right now. Hungry."

Hawker watched as the woman stood abruptly and stripped the cotton gown over her head. It was the same ripe, earth-brown body he had seen that afternoon, but the firelight added subtleties of shape and texture that made her look even more desirable. Suddenly shy with the vigilante's eyes hard on her, she gave a girlish shrug, "I know I ain't much to look at anymore. Having babies puts some wear on a woman's body. But what I got, Mr. Hawker, is all yours, yours to do as you want, any way you want. All I ask is that you treat me like a woman. Tell me what to do, and I'll do it."

Hawker took the woman by the shoulders and pulled her to him, sliding his hands down so they cupped her large, soft breasts. "For starters, how about calling me James?"

Her head was thrown back, eyes slightly closed. "That surely does feel nice, James," she moaned.

Hawker lowered her breasts down onto his face, feeling the nipples flatten themselves against his eyes. Then he began to use his tongue on her, touching her nipples in slow rhythm to the pressure her hips made against his bare leg.

He rolled her over then, and she pulled his lips to hers, hard, as her hands moved over his body and stripped away his underwear, and Hawker wrapped his fists in her long black

33

hair as her legs spread wide and, with her small left hand, she found him and guided him into her, too anxious for any more touching or hugging, hungry, as she had said, for the feel of a man in her.

Her face had gone soft and sluggish, her eyes closed, lips swollen, and she moaned in ecstasy with each thrust the vigilante made as the sweat from his forehead dripped down onto her face.

His left arm, he noticed, had begun to bleed again.

It was more than an hour before Hawker had time to do anything about it.

When Hawker first awoke, he wasn't so sure that it all hadn't been a dream. But the quick, familiar kiss Lomela gave him told him it had been real enough.

"How's your fever, James?"

"All gone, Lomela. How's *your* fever?"

She flashed a vampish smile. "Never better. I found me the sure cure for it last night"—her smile broadened—"but it's only a temporary cure."

"I'm happy to hear that. My body's happy, too—I think." Grimacing humorously, Hawker got up and wrapped the blanket around himself as Lomela returned to the wood stove where thick slices of bacon and a half-dozen eggs were frying in the same black skillet. "Where are your kids?"

The woman pointed with the spatula. "I sent my girl, Dolores, for a bucket of water. My oldest, K.D.—he's nine—is out chopping me some more wood so I can finish your breakfast."

Hawker's expression changed as he went quickly to the

window. He pulled back the deerskin curtain. "How long have they been gone?"

"'Bout five minutes." The woman handed him a cup of very dark coffee as she asked quickly, "Don't you see them out there?"

Hawker dropped the curtain back, smiling. "I see them. They're fine. Good-looking kids, too. I thought so yesterday, watching them through the binoculars."

The woman came into Hawker's arms, smiling. "The way you watched me?"

"I could have lied to you. I could have said I was a gentleman and turned away."

She slid her hand up under the blanket and held him in her fingers as she gave him a quick kiss. "I'm glad Tom Dulles didn't send no gentleman to watch over us. Maybe that man really does still care about me."

Hawker found the clothes he had worn under the camouflaged jump suit: jeans, black crew-neck sweater, ankle-high climbing boots with Vibram soles. When he was dressed, he sat at the plank table while the woman served him the bacon and eggs. "You're going to have to leave here with me, Lomela. You know that, don't you? We're going to have to leave today."

"I know. I'm kind of disappointed, too. I surely do like this cabin. It was kind of lonely the first week, but then the kids and me got to liking it. The air's so pure and the mountains are so pretty—"

"And Bill Nek's men know exactly where it is. When those four goons don't report back in, Nek is going to order another one of his hit squads up here to see what happened. I don't want you and your kids waiting around to be questioned. While I'm taking care of my business up there on the mountainside this morning, you and your kids get packed. We'll load your gear onto that Appaloosa mare and walk out. I've got a Land Cruiser hidden on a logging trail about three miles from here. I'll drive you back to Denver, we'll get in touch with Tom Dulles, and we'll decide on a new hiding place for you."

As she took Hawker's empty plate, she hesitated and looked at him closely. "But what will you do—after that, I mean?"

"I've got to find where Nek is hiding Jimmy Estes and Chuck Phillips. I think that's the key to this whole operation. That's probably where Nek keeps most of his hired guns and most of his illegal munitions. When they took your father there, they made sure he was blindfolded. And when he escaped, it was dark, and they'd worn him half-crazy, so about all he can remember is that their hideout is in a deserted silver mine in a high valley not far from Leadville."

"There's no shortage of high valleys around Leadville," the woman said. "Finding one little played-out silver mine could take you months."

"I'll stay however long I have to stay and do whatever I have to do to find them. We have a couple of things working in our favor. Nek has to keep your father and his two partners alive. If one of them dies, then the trust awards the remaining shares of stock to you—but in the form of a yearly allowance that would make it impossible for you to sell to anybody. Nek knows that. His lawyers have made sure he knows it. So Nek has to come up with some kind of leverage so strong that he can convince your father and his two partners to sell. I don't doubt that he can do that, but it'll take time. And with every hour that goes by, I'll be that much closer to him and his gang."

"But why is it, you think, Mr. Nek wants my daddy's mine so bad? He's got all the money he could ever need. He's got an estate in Denver as big as a castle—I've seen it from the road. And he's got about a dozen condos in Aspen and Snowmass. Anything that man wants, he can afford to buy."

Hawker shrugged. "Maybe you just put your finger on it— part of it, at least. Maybe Nek doesn't like the idea of his old partners having something he wants but can't buy. Maybe it touches some of the old guilt he feels. Put yourself in his place. Fifty years ago, you cheat your three best friends out of a lot of money. You come up with some shoddy way to rationalize it: all's fair in love and business, that sort of thing. Even so, the guilt is always there, always lingering just beneath the surface. So you go a little crazy, and you dedicate your whole life to making money, acquiring silver. You want to prove to your-self and everyone else that you really are the Silver King—not because of what you stole from your friends but because of your ability to accumulate a fortune. And didn't Nek prove that, in a way? Compared with the wealth he's amassed, that little bit he stole from his partners fifty years ago is really just a drop in the bucket. But your dad and the other two guys still remained broken-down old prospectors—in Nek's eyes, anyway. Don't you see how that could justify his actions in his own mind? He didn't steal the money. He *deserved* it by virtue of being the only one of the four to be able to handle the money successfully. But then suddenly his old partners weren't just broken-down old prospectors anymore. Nek got news that they had struck a deep vein—a vein that might rival the wealth of any of the mines he owns. Naturally, he wants it. He can't allow the actions of his entire life to be proven wrong. He can't let his old partners do better than he's done."

The woman listened quietly. "I never thought about it like that before," she said. "I just always pictured Mr. Nek as being a pure nasty mean man."

"Maybe he is," Hawker said. "Hell, he *probably* is. Could be he just wants to corner the silver market—he wouldn't be the first to try it. But one thing's for sure: when Bill Nek wants something, he'll stop at nothing to get it. Murder, kidnapping, whatever it takes. And when a man has as much money as he has, the only way to fight him is to use his own tactics. That's just what I plan to do when I find his—"

Hawker's words were interrupted by a shrill scream—then another.

Lomela dropped the pan she had been washing. "Dolores! My god, they've got my babies!"

Hawker grabbed the Colt Commando from the corner and went crashing through the doorway outside. He got a quick glimpse of the black-haired girl being carried off toward the woods, kicking and screaming, over a man's shoulder. The man was wearing a green coverall snowsuit. Then another man stepped into view and squeezed off two quick shots from a shotgun. Hawker dropped to the ground. At that distance, the pellets fell far short of him. The vigilante raised the Commando to fire, then reconsidered. There was too great a chance of hitting the girl—and he had no idea where the boy was.

As he got to his feet, Lomela went running past him,

screaming. Hawker grabbed her from behind and wrestled her to the ground. She had the strength of a bobcat, and it took him a few moments to subdue her.

"Lomela! Listen to me! They want you to follow, don't you understand? They want to take you hostage, too—"

"But I want to be with my babies!" she cried.

"Is it worth getting one of them, or even both of them killed? Until they have you, they have to take good care of those kids. But once they do have you, the kids are expend-able. Understand?"

The woman stopped struggling. She looked up into Hawk-er's face, her eyes wide with sheer terror. "I'll do what you say, James. I'll do anything you say. But please—*please* get my little boy and girl back. You have to do that for me. You have to promise me—"

Hawker was helping the woman to her feet, calming her as best he could. She grabbed him by the sweater and shook him. "Don't just say you'll do it! Promise that you will get my children back, damn it!"

The vigilante stepped away, holding her at arm's distance. "Do you know what you're saying? Do you know what you're asking me to do? If I go after those kids now, it'll double the danger they're in. And they're already in enough danger."

"I can't let that *scum* keep my children, James. Can't you understand that? My kids are going to be scared out of their wits! It may change them for the rest of their lives. You have to get them back before it's too late!"

Hawker nodded. "Okay," he said. "I'll go after them on one condition."

"Anything. Anything at all. Just tell me what you want."

"I want you to stay by my side. I want you to do exactly what I tell you to do without question. Understand?"

The woman nodded meekly.

Hawker took a deep breath. His left arm was throbbing again and, after just that little bit of activity, he was already feeling weak. "Okay," he said. "If you've got a saddle, stick it on that horse, and make it quick. We've got to catch them before they get to their vehicle. Did you hear the sound of any kind of motor this morning?"

The woman shook her head immediately. "No, and I listened, too. Their truck or Jeep can't be very close."

"Good," said Hawker, returning to the cabin for the rest of his weaponry. "Let's go."

FIVE

Hawker swung up onto the big Appaloosa mare and pulled Lomela onto the cantle behind him.

"Are you sure you know how to ride?" the woman cried.

"I know enough to know I'm not very good at it," snapped Hawker, who did not like or trust horses. "Just shut up and hang on. And no matter what happens, don't drop that canvas backpack."

"You already have the terrible-looking machine gun strapped to the saddle. Why do you need this backpack?"

"Because that thing strapped to the saddle is an automatic rifle, not a machine gun, and I thought you weren't going to ask any questions."

"But this backpack is so heavy—"

"It's heavy because of the grenades."

The woman's voice dropped to a whisper. "Oh, my god."

Hawker kicked the horse into a canter and was immediately relieved to find that the animal was smooth-gaited. That meant that there was a good chance he might not fall off at all.

RANDY WAYNE WHITE

He tried to remember the emergency riding lessons a Texas Ranger friend of his had given him one Mexican night long, long ago: back straight, reins in the left hand, knees turned inward, ass lifting and falling slightly with the horse, not fighting the horse.

Even when he did it right, he felt like a subject in a hemorrhoid experiment.

The vigilante reined the horse toward the river, and the animal charged through the icy water and up onto the grassy plain beyond.

"They didn't go this way!" the woman called into his ear. "They went the other way."

"I know that!" Hawker yelled back. "And if I have to remind you not to ask questions one more time, I'm going to throw your ass right off this horse—I mean that, Lomela!"

The woman lapsed into a moody silence behind him.

Hawker steered the horse up the side of the mountain toward the nearest pass. He continued to press the animal to run, for he knew that they didn't have more than a couple of miles to go. No matter where the kidnappers had parked, they still had to take the logging trail out. And his only chance of taking them was when they passed by.

At the top of the pass, Hawker almost reined up. The view was stunning. The great Colorado Rockies moved away through the clouds like waves, one after another, silver mountains touched with veins of white and green against the pale blue sky.

The horse grunted as Hawker nudged it with his heels, urging it down the slope.

At a stand of aspens, Hawker stopped abruptly. "Get off," he said.

The woman was surprised. "What? Those men aren't here. They can't be anywhere around here."

"I know that," said Hawker. "That's why I want you off here. If I bungle the rescue attempt on your children, I don't want them to get you, too. Understand?"

"But couldn't I help you in some way—"

"Lomela," Hawker said impatiently, "let me explain something to you. Getting your kids back is not going to be easy, but I am going to give it my best try. I am not up here on a lark. I am here because I do what I do very damn well. And I don't like to do anything on a whim, because whims are dangerous, and in my business they get the wrong people killed. I'm a planner and a plotter. I think everything out ahead—*everything*. It's like a curse, see? So when I tell you to do something, it's not because I'm trying to be mean or because I'm mad at my astrologer. It's because I damn well *want* you to do it, and I don't like to be questioned every step of the way. Questions are a waste of time, and things that waste time can get people killed. Understood?"

The woman slid down off the horse. "Should I wait here?" she asked meekly.

"Yes, you should wait here. Even if the kidnappers zap me and start a search for you, they won't find you here. When it's safe for you to come down to the logging trail, I'll fire four shots: the middle two will be close together. If you don't hear that signal within the next hour, beat it down the mountain to the nearest phone and give Tom Dulles a call." The vigilante allowed himself to smile slightly. "Don't worry, Lomela. I'll do the very best I can to free those handsome kids of yours."

Close to tears, the woman nodded quickly. "I'm sorry I'm so much trouble, but I'm just so worried about them I can't think straight—"

Hawker reined the horse away. "You already made it up to me—last night."

Then he and the horse were lunging down the slope. Hawker kept both hands firmly on the saddle horn and his feet well-braced in the stirrups as the Appaloosa twisted in and out of the pale yellow aspen trees. Then he could see the logging trail just ahead. It was an overgrown, twisting, turning ribbon that worked its way precariously down the mountain.

Hawker knew that because he had driven up it the previous day. His own vehicle was about a mile to the south, well-hidden by the branches of a red pine with which he had covered it.

Hawker got down off the horse and led it to an area just above the logging trail. He tied the horse out of view, then set about trying to find something with which to block the path. There were boulders around, but none were small enough to be moved by a man with a wounded arm. There were a few fallen trees, but they were too large, too. Finally, he found a partially rotted tree trunk that looked as if it might be big enough, and he dragged it laboriously across the trail.

Then he climbed up the embankment, found his Colt Commando and his knapsack, and settled himself in some bushes and waited. The kidnappers had headed west from the cabin, so he expected them to come charging down the narrow trail at any moment.

Even so, it was nearly ten minutes before he finally heard the high-torque whine of the four-wheel-drive Wagoneer coming from around the bend. Hawker got to his knees, the Commando ready. What he hoped to do was zap the first man as he got out to move the tree, then immediately nail the second as he sat waiting behind the wheel.

The plan had a couple of flaws, not the least of which was the fact that the Commando was an assault rifle built for tough action in cramped quarters, not accuracy over any great distance. If the two children were anywhere within the sighting area, he wouldn't be able to fire at all.

As it turned out, though, that was not the plan's greatest flaw. The plan's greatest flaw was that the man driving the Wagoneer decided not to stop for the fallen tree. Hawker heard the man downshift and hit the gas in preparation for jumping the log, and he knew immediately that there was only one thing he could do. He got to his feet, waited until the vehicle had already jolted over the tree, then jumped spread-eagle onto the luggage rack on the roof of the car.

Immediately, there was a shattering roar as a bullet gouged a hole in the roof of the car. Hawker rolled to the side just as far as he could as two more ugly spouts appeared in the roof.

From inside the Jeep, Hawker could hear the children screaming. He had to make this quick if any of them were going to survive.

In one swift motion, he locked his toes into the luggage

rack and leaned his head down over the passenger's window, the stout little assault rifle in his right hand. The man in the passenger's seat looked shocked as the vigilante touched the barrel to his head.

"Throw it out the window before I drill you a new ear!" Hawker yelled.

He could see Lomela's little girl and boy cringing in the backseat as the man let the husky .45-caliber ACP drop from his finger out the window.

The dumb expression never left his big ugly face. Hawker turned the barrel toward the driver. "You too, buddy," he yelled. "Take your weapon out of that shoulder holster with your left hand. Use two fingers. Drop it out the window."

The driver began to reach toward the automatic in the shoulder holster, but then his eyes hardened and he twisted the wheel suddenly. The jolt almost flung Hawker off the roof. "Try that again," the vigilante yelled, "and I'll put a bullet through your knee!"

"And get these two brats killed?" the man hollered back. "You won't do it. You don't have the balls!"

The driver swerved again, and Hawker had to tighten his grip and clamp his legs. Now they were on a portion of road that lurched back and forth down the side of the mountain, and the vigilante found himself looking out over a sheer drop of several hundred feet. If the driver made a mistake, it would mean death for all of them.

Inside, the children cried out again as the Wagoneer slid precariously close to the edge of the cliff.

Hawker could hardly force himself to look.

There was another explosion, and the roof was pocked once more by a bullet hole.

They were shooting at him again.

He had to do something, and do it soon.

The vigilante slid the Commando under his right thigh, pressing tightly, locked his toes under the luggage rack again, and swung out over the window of the driver's side. With one quick motion, he grabbed the door handle in his aching left hand and the hair of the driver's head in his right hand.

The passenger now had the driver's handgun and was bringing it up to fire!

Hawker yanked the driver out of the vehicle, his ears indifferent to the hideous scream the man gave as he tumbled toward the ledge and certain death.

The Jeep gave a sickening lunge toward the cliff, but now the passenger grabbed the wheel and slid over in front of the controls, as Hawker had been certain he would. When he felt the vehicle come back under control, he swung back down on the passenger's side and poked the assault rifle at the new driver. "Toss your weapon out the window, friend, or I'll blow your nose off!"

"I don't think you have the nerve!" the driver retorted, but the anxious look on his face said very plainly that he did think Hawker had the nerve.

Hawker raised the weapon as if to fire. "Okay, buddy, okay!" the man cried as he threw the brutal-looking handgun out the window. "Just don't shoot me!"

RANDY WAYNE WHITE

"Pull this Jeep to the side—now! Do everything slow and easy!"

The man steered the Wagoneer toward the wooded side of the logging trail, then braked to a stop. Hawker took a long breath of relief. His toes were cramped from trying to bury themselves in the metal of the roof. He continued to point the automatic rifle at the man as he said, "Okay, sport, slide out from behind that wheel and keep your hands high. Now fold your hands behind your head and kick the door closed with your boot. Good, now touch your nose to that tree. If you so much as move, you'll join your friend at the bottom of that gorge."

Hawker got to his feet, stepped down onto the hood of the vehicle, and jumped to the ground. The children were now sitting quietly in the backseat. Their faces were pale and they looked very glum.

Hawker looked in the window and smiled. "Dolores? K.D.? Are you two all right?"

They both had onyx-black hair, like their mother. The little boy's hair was Indian-straight, but the girl's hair had some curl. "That man fell off the cliff back there," K.D. said gravely.

"That's something you had absolutely nothing to do with," the vigilante said gently. "Those men were wrong to make you go riding with them. But it's not your fault. I'm going to take you home to your mother now."

"I'll bet Mommy is worried," said the little girl.

"That's right," said the vigilante, "your mother is worried. We need to hurry. Everything will be okay now. Can you two just sit right here for a few minutes more? I won't be long."

The kidnapper in the green snowsuit still stood with his

nose against the tree. Hawker went to him and touched the barrel of the Commando to the back of his head. "You and I are going to have a long talk, sport," he said. "I'd like to have that talk right now. There are a lot of questions I need answered. But I hate to see those kids kept away from their mother any longer. After the stunt you and your dead friend just pulled, they'll probably be having nightmares until they're well into high school anyway—"

"It wasn't my idea to snatch the kids. I was just following my orders."

"Whose orders? Bill Nek's?"

"I can't tell you anything about that," the man said nervously. "A guy like you's been around. You know what the score is in things like this. If I spill my guts, the people I work for will make sure I get a hand hacked off or something like that. Don't make me talk—"

"There's nobody around but you and me, is there? Who would ever know that you talked?"

"They'd know," the man said anxiously. "They got all kinds of ways of knowing. That's why I can't tell you nothin', mister. I just can't—"

"Oh, you'll talk," Hawker said easily. "By the time I get done with you, you'll tell me more than I want to know. In fact, I've just thought of a way to soften you up."

Quickly, Hawker pulled two lengths of rope from his backpack. He used the shortest section to bind the man's hands and arms behind his back. Then he took the hundred-foot length and tied a rescuer's bowline around the man's chest. He tied the other end securely to a tree.

"Let's go," Hawker said, pushing him roughly out of sight of the children and toward the precipice where the logging trail dropped off several hundred feet to rocks below.

"What are you going to do?" the man yelled. "My god, you're not going to push me off—"

"I want to make sure you're here when I get back, sport," Hawker said, shoving him along. "Dangling over the gorge might help convince you that I mean business."

The man was almost crying now. "Okay, okay, I'll talk, just don't make me—"

"I've got to take the kids back, friend. Do you know what I think the lowest thing in this world is? It's an adult who would intentionally hurt a child. That's just what you've done, sport. Now you're going to hang over this ledge until I get back and haul your ass up."

Hawker gave him a light shove, and the man screamed as Hawker began to lower him down over the gorge. "I'm afraid of heights, for Christ's sake!"

"No kidding," said Hawker peering down over the ledge as the man swung back and forth like a pendulum. "You're not going to like this at all then, are you?"

Hawker fired off the four-shot signal, then drove the Wagoneer back along the logging trail until he saw Lomela hurrying along the path toward them. The reunion between the mother and her two children was joyful. Hawker felt as if he really had done some good. He gave the woman the keys to the Jeep and told her to drive back to the cabin and get packed. He'd pick up the Appaloosa, question the man, then meet them on the logging trail for the trip back to Denver.

There was only one hitch in the plan.

When Hawker, now on horseback, returned to the precipice, he found that the man was gone.

At first, he couldn't believe it.

But then he saw that someone had cut the rope.

SIX

Tom Dulles was a lanky, lean, rank-haired man in his mid-thirties who had been a Denver cop for ten years. He had grown up on a scraggly cattle ranch on the Utah side of Rangely, Colorado, a sagebrush town dotted with bars and oil rigs. He had attended the junior college at Rangely, played baseball under Paul "Snuffy" Conrad, then gone on to major in law enforcement at the University of Denver. When his alcoholic father died, he returned to Rangely, sold the family holdings for next to nothing—which was what the family holdings were worth—then went back to the Mile High City to seek a new life.

That was during what was known as the Hippie Era in Denver. The long-haired children of America's affluent roamed the streets begging for dimes, planning revolts, cheering Tom Hayden's support of North Vietnam's systematic slaughter of American "war criminals," dropping acid, doing group sex, and tripping their brains out during demonstrations in Washington Park.

Dulles, who had grown up as a rangehand shitkicker, had no politics, but he was smart enough to know that he could get into the pants of most of the blond-haired hippie debutantes for the price of an anti-Nixon remark. His sexual activity increased in direct proportion to his political activism. He began a marathon sampler of white girls, black girls, teenyboppers, Eastern intellectuals, and California beauties who loved herbal shampoos and synthetic drugs. Only a really virulent case of the clap kept him from running for public office.

It was while recovering that Dulles began to understand some of the political horseshit he had been spouting. Within a week, he had joined the Marines. He was shipped to Nam, spent a month scared shitless that he was going to be killed, spent another ten months scared he *wasn't* going to be killed, then two more months in Saigon recovering from a case of Asiatic clap that made the American version seem uninteresting.

When he returned to the world, he joined the Denver P.D. He became a happily married, happily settled citizen of Colorado. But then his young wife had slumped over one afternoon at the dinner table, and he spent the next three years in and out of hospitals. He had the affair with Lomela, broke off the affair with Lomela, and now was tending to his convalescing wife and his job as a police lieutenant.

It was this man whom James Hawker now sat across the table from in a ritzy San Francisco—style bar in downtown Denver, a man Hawker liked instinctively. Within a few minutes, each man trusted the other without reservation. Dulles wore a conservative gray suit and blue tie, and he was drinking Scotch, neat. Hawker was munching fried potato skins and sipping at his tankard of Coors.

"I really appreciate what you did for Lomela," Dulles was saying. "That business with the goons who kidnapped her kids sounded pretty hairy. She told me all about it."

Hawker raised his eyebrows. "She told you everything?"

A mild smile crossed Dulles's face. "What she didn't tell me, she implied. I like that woman; I like her a lot. For a while, I thought I loved her. God knows, she sure helped me when I was down. She's that rare breed: simple, tough, hardworking, and she takes a lot of enjoyment in being a woman."

"A rare breed," Hawker agreed.

"If you two have something going, I'm all for it."

"It was more like first aid," the vigilante replied. "But I'm glad you're not upset. She still cares about you, and I don't want to get caught in the middle of anything."

"You won't. I'm just happy as hell that you were there to help. Look, you don't have to tell me, but I'd like to know. What did you do to scare off Nek's gunmen? I mean, I know some of those assholes. They're drug-blitzed. They have no minds anymore. They'll do absolutely anything that Nek tells them to do. It's not that they're fearless as much as that they're too burned out to know what fear is. So if you've got a way of scaring them, I'd really like to know it."

Hawker looked at him blankly. "Scare them? I didn't scare them."

"But Lomela said—"

"Lomela lied because she didn't want me to get into trouble."

Dulles's dark eyes narrowed in reappraisal. "Then how did you get rid of them?"

Hawker finished his beer and held the pewter mug up as a signal to the waitress. The waitress wore a scarlet dance-hall dress and feathers in her hair. "Tom," the vigilante said easily, "you're a bright guy. The reason you happened to know about me was because I've built a reputation for solving problems that regular law-enforcement agencies can't touch. I didn't build that reputation because I'm a better cop than the average municipal cop. I built it because I go ahead and do what no other cop can legally do. It's the only real advantage I have. Several years ago, I decided I'd had enough of the bureaucratic bullshit. I decided that this nation had a real need for someone trained in law enforcement who wasn't afraid to cut corners, someone who wasn't afraid to play judge, jury, and executioner. But when I made that decision, I also knew that anyone who knew the details of my missions could, in a legal sense, become an accomplice." Hawker took the tankard of beer from the waitress, exchanging a dollar tip for her warm smile. "So now I'm going to ask you again. Do you really want to know what I did to scare those guys off, Tom?"

Dulles nodded. "Like you said, I've been around, Hawk. I don't mind taking a few chances myself. So tell me before I threaten to turn you in to the *Post*."

Hawker shrugged. "I killed them."

"What?"

"I killed them—all of them except one, that is. Someone else killed that one, but I have no idea who."

Dulles gave a low whistle. "You actually greased the dinks who came after Lomela? How many?"

"Six in all; five by my hand."

Dulles took a long drink of his Scotch. "You know, the guys down at the P.D. used to talk about you, in the gym or the steam room—you know, bullshit talk. They had heard rumors like you'd blown away fifteen or twenty street punks in L.A., or a dozen New York hoods, or an army of revolutionaries. Stuff like that. I never believed it because who in the hell could get away with stuff like that? They said your trick was to never ever waste anybody who didn't deserve it. They said if we got a scramble call on some dude who has greased Denver's three biggest heroin pushers, how fast are we really going to scramble? After we shake his hand and buy him a few beers, we might tell him to get his ass in gear before someone from the ACLU comes along and nails us all." Dulles smiled a crooked, Gary Cooper kind of smile. "So now I find out the rumors weren't all bullshit. I learn you really do pack the terrible swift sword."

Hawker chuckled. "I've heard those same rumors, and I can tell you right now that a lot of them are bullshit. They make me out to be stronger than a locomotive and faster than a speeding bullet." He motioned to his stiff left arm. "But I almost got wasted two nights ago because I was dumb and didn't keep track of some asshole with a knife in the dark. I've had my butt kicked more than once, and all too often I'd like to kick my own butt for being just plain stupid. But you don't hear the stories about my screw-ups"—Hawker smiled wryly—"and I guess I'm glad. Any well-trained cop could do what I do if he had the weaponry and the financial backing and the go-for-broke attitude. That's the real difference: the go-for-broke attitude. The killers and the rapists and the crooks don't expect it. I mean, who in the hell can really chase them like they deserve to be chased? An honest cop can't. The courts wouldn't let him even if his work schedule allowed it. So when someone finally does, it shocks the hell out of them. They get real nervous. They make stupid mistakes. And with me, they don't get a chance to be a repeat offender."

"So you really did waste six of Big Bill Nek's gunmen," Dulles said in a tone of amused wonderment. "Boy, is he going to be pissed."

"I eliminated five," Hawker corrected. "I tied the sixth one to a rope and dropped him over a cliff—"

"You what?"

"I didn't let him hit the ground. I just dropped him part of the way. I wanted information from him. I wanted him to know I meant business."

"That would certainly convince me you meant business."

"I was gone for about half an hour," Hawker said, "and when I got back I found that somebody had cut the rope."

"Who in the hell could have done that? Do you think maybe he climbed back up, cut the rope, and split?"

Hawker shook his head. "He split, all right. I could see him lying on the rocks below. Somebody came by and decided he needed the Isaac Newton cure for insomnia. I have no idea who. But whoever did it was bleeding. There was blood on the rope. He must have cut himself. I'm not worried about that now, though. Now I need to find Nek's mountain hideaway. Where is he keeping Jimmy Estes and Chuck Phillips hostage?"

"Well, you know the official line is that Estes and Phillips were up in the mountains and just disappeared. We have absolutely no proof that they were kidnapped. The P.D. doesn't even have anyone working on the case; in fact, there is no case. But if I were looking for Estes and Phillips, I'd get old Robert Carthay to try to lead me back to that abandoned mine. I know it was dark when he escaped, and I know he was half-crazy, but that man knows the Colorado Rockies better than anyone I've ever met, and I think the route is stuck somewhere in his subconscious. Hell, I'd bet on it."

Hawker thought for a moment, shaking his head slowly. "But Nek probably had Estes and Phillips moved to a different location after Carthay escaped," he said. "I think Carthay is better off hidden in the mountains. No, we have to think of some other way to find out."

"We could get topographical maps, pick out the most likely areas, then get a chopper to fly us around," said Dulles.

"It may come to that. But I have something I'd like to try first. You said Nek has a big place here in Denver, didn't you?"

"He's the richest man in town, and he has the biggest estate. It's just outside Englewood."

Hawker finished his beer. "Why don't we drive there right now and ask Nek where he's keeping them?"

Dulles laughed, but his laughter slowly faded when he noticed the look in the vigilante's gray eyes. "You're serious, aren't you?"

Hawker dropped a ten-dollar bill onto the table. "Don't worry. This will be a friendly visit."

SEVEN

Bill Nek didn't live on an estate. He lived in a fortress that was built on a park grounds that ended abruptly at the edge of a cliff that towered over the Denver skyline.

Because Tom Dulles drove, it was Dulles who talked to the armed guard at the black wrought-iron gate.

Leaning into the window, the guard asked, "Do you have an appointment to see Mr. Nek?"

"I don't think he's expecting us," Dulles said, looking at Hawker for confirmation.

"Then could you kindly state your business," said the guard with an imperious air.

Hawker leaned toward the window. "Get on the phone and tell Nek we're here to talk about the sale of the Chiquita Silver Mine." The sharpness of Hawker's tone set the guard back a step.

"Silver mine, sir," he said. "Yes, sir. I'll be right back, sir."

The guard stepped through the pedestrian gate and disappeared into a small stone house. A few minutes later, he reappeared. "Mr. Nek will send a car for you," the guard said.

"What do you think we're sitting in?" Dulles laughed. "We'd rather drive ourselves."

The guard could not be swayed. "If you wish to see Mr. Nek, you will take the car they send for you. There can be no exceptions. Please park on the asphalt space to the right, then step through the gate, please. The car will be here in a few minutes."

The car was a black Cadillac limo with tinted windows, television antenna, armor plating, and a carriage as long as a bus. Before Hawker and Dulles could get in, three big men in business suits jumped out and approached them.

"Christ," Dulles whispered to Hawker, "they look like the CIA."

"I hope not," Hawker said wryly. "The CIA has spent the last two years trying to kill me."

Dulles looked at him blankly. "You could have told me that before I let you get into my car."

"You're the one who said he didn't mind taking a few chances."

Dulles grimaced. "Shit, I'm traveling with a marked man."

"We'd like to ask you gentlemen a few questions before you see Mr. Nek," the biggest of the three men said with a trace of a European accent. Like the others, he wore dark aviator sunglasses, and he had very short hair. These three were of a different breed from the drug-damaged killers Hawker had faced in the mountains. These guys were cool, calculating professionals. The spokesman was German, judging by his accent. He operated with German thoroughness. Each of them had a look of icy detachment that suggested they would kill with the same dedication to efficiency they probably gave to their physical training and to their dress styles.

This was Nek's first team, his personal guard. Hawker knew there would be no bullshitting these guys. Germans, unlike the buffoons on *Hogan's Heroes*, did not fool easily or kindly.

"Would you two gentlemen mind standing against the automobile?" the biggest man asked. He had pure white hair and hands the size of bowling balls. His questions weren't questions, they were orders.

"Are you going to shoot us or search us?" Hawker asked easily.

None of the three men smiled. "If you wish to speak with Mr. Nek, you must first be searched," the big German said.

"I'll bet he has a hell of a time getting his phones fixed," the vigilante said as he assumed the spread-eagle position against the limo.

The men used hand-held metal detectors, going over both Hawker and Dulles thoroughly. "Wouldn't it have been easier to ask me for my weapons?" Hawker quipped as the Beretta was removed from the holster strapped to his right ankle and the Randall survival knife was taken from the scabbard on his left ankle.

"Dis man has a badge," one of the men said in a very heavy accent as he looked at Dulles's billfold.

"All cops have badges," said Dulles. "It's kind of like belonging to a club."

Once again, no smiles.

"Are you here on police business?"

"No. We're here to talk about a silver mine," Hawker replied.

"Then why do you come armed?"

"Because a friend told us we'd disappoint the hell out of

Nek's security team if we didn't." Hawker smiled. "See how much fun you're having?"

The big German scowled as he went to the car, spoke on the phone, then returned. "Mr. Nek has agreed to see you. You will sit in the back between my two associates. Your weapons will be returned to you upon the completion of your interview."

The ride was like a funeral procession. Hawker had to fight the childish urge to giggle. From the way Dulles refused to look at him, he was sure the Denver cop felt the same way. The two-lane asphalt drive twisted through an estate of rolling hills, aspen stands, rushing streams, and neat, golf-green lawns. The house was four stories high, ivy on white stone, with a weird cubical symmetry, as if it had been designed by an architect from the late 1950s. There was an eight-car garage and a walkway along the top of the house, like a bastion mount. Off to the left, through the silver aspens, Hawker saw a wind sock, and he knew there was a runway nearby.

"Follow me," said the German. He led them up broad stone stairs, through double doors, into the most garishly decorated place Hawker had ever seen. The carpet was glowing burgundy, the walls some kind of furry crepe, and the furniture was a mixture of modern glass and stainless steel, early American, and Archie Bunker Salvation Army. It was part whorehouse, part model home, part middle-class suburbia.

"Christ," Dulles whispered, "it looks like a tornado hit a couple of mobile home parks and a fag bar before dumping everything here."

"Mr. Nek is in the library," intoned the German.

Another set of double doors opened, and Hawker got his first look at Nek. The old man stood facing him, wearing a blazing red smoking jacket and holding a tawdry paperback in his hand. He had a craggy hawk face with bushy white eyebrows, tiny, fierce blue eyes, and skin as pale as parchment. His mouth was turned perpetually down at the corners, as if something nearby smelled foul. He was still a big man, but he had clearly once been bigger. His shoulders were slumped with age, and his big hands were gnarled. There was a withered, bitter look to the man as if he were drying up rather than growing old. Not that he looked incapacitated; he didn't. Nek still had the manner of someone who was still very much in control, a glowering attitude that the vigilante had seen in the eyes of convicted killers. He stood by a window that allowed no light to enter. Like all the others, it was sealed by heavy green drapes. Were it not for the fire and the overhead light, the room would have been in utter darkness. Nek studied Hawker, looked at Dulles, then motioned roughly to chairs by the roaring fire. He said with an edge, "If you two messenger boys have something to say, sit down and make it quick. I'm a busy man."

Hawker took a chair while Dulles remained standing. "Doesn't a good host usually offer his guests something to drink?" Hawker asked easily.

The man glared at the vigilante. "Listen to me, you little punk. I let you in here because you said you had something to say about the Chiquita Mine. If you do, you'd better spit it out. If not, I can have the two of you carried out in a bag if I like." He had taken a step closer and was shaking his finger at the vigilante. "And one more thing, punk. When you talk to me, you call me sir. I don't give a flying fuck if you're a Denver cop or not. I own more cops than you own socks."

Hawker looked at Dulles with a bored expression on his face. "Is he trying to put me in my place? Or is he just practicing his vocabulary?"

Dulles picked up on the tone of Hawker's voice. "I think he's just trying to get his heart beating," Dulles said. "It looks like the poor old fart has been dead for the last two or three hours."

The vigilante looked at the man known as the Silver King, the most ruthless man in Colorado. "For one thing, Nek, I'm not a cop. My name is Hawker. James Hawker. Maybe you've heard of me. If you haven't, then I know you'll remember that a couple of days ago you sent a half-dozen of your goons into the mountains to kidnap Lomela Carthay and her two children. But your goons haven't come back yet, have they? And do you know what? They never will come back, Nek. They'll never come back because I killed them."

The color had slowly drained from Nek's face. But he did a good job of hiding the shock he clearly felt. "I don't know what the fuck you're talking about, Hawker. If you've come up here to try to snow me, it won't work. Better men than you have tried it, and I've buried each and every one of them—figuratively, of course." His eyes glittered as if to say he wasn't speaking at all figuratively. "Now, if you really have murdered some men, then, as a respected citizen of Denver, I think it's only fair to warn you that it's my duty to notify the authorities."

The vigilante shrugged. "There's a phone on the desk. Go ahead and call them. I'll wait right here."

Nek put down the book he had been reading and walked toward the phone. Hawker said, "When the cops get here, maybe you can explain to them why you kidnapped your old partners Jimmy Estes and Chuck Phillips, and why Robert Carthay was half-crazy after he managed to escape from your goons."

Nek hesitated. "I have no idea what you're talking about," he said.

"Oh, no? Then how about this: maybe I'll have the cops ask why you have the bandage on your hand."

The man touched his hand reflexively, as if to cover the bandage. "I was working in the garden and cut myself," Nek said testily.

"Bullshit," snapped Hawker. "You killed one of your own men two days ago up in the mountains. He was hanging over a cliff and you cut the rope because you heard him agree to tell me about you and your operation."

It jarred the old man. His face paled, and he sat down in a chair by the fire, no longer interested in calling the police. It jarred him, but it didn't beat him, and he sure as hell wasn't intimidated. "That's the wildest tale I've ever heard, Hawker. I suppose you plan on lying to the cops. Maybe tell them you saw me cut the rope, huh?"

"I could tell them that. Or I could tell them I saw your boots there drying by the fire, and that I noticed that the lacings are covered with the same kind of beggar lice that got on my boots while I was in that valley. Or I could tell them that the killer was left-handed and he gashed his right hand with the knife while he was cutting the rope." Hawker nodded. "That's how you got that bandage on your hand, isn't it?"

Nek had recovered his poise. "Just an unfortunate gardening accident," he smiled. "I have a dozen people who saw me cut my hand on a machete."

Hawker shrugged. "Then I guess I would have to tell the police that I saw you cut the rope. Makes no difference to me. I don't mind lying. We have that in common, don't we, Nek? Neither of us minds lying."

The old man's face had turned so red it was nearly purple. His voice quivered as he spoke, "Listen to me, you nasty young motherfucker. Twenty years ago, I'd have kicked your little pink ass for talking to me like that—"

"You were a coward twenty years ago, too, Nek," Hawker interrupted. "What were you then? Fifty? Maybe a little younger? People who are cowards stay cowards. You didn't have the guts to face up to your three partners after you stole their silver claim. Hell, you don't even have the nerve to face up to them now. So spare me that shit about what you would have done twenty years ago."

"You think the Denver D.A. would take your word over mine, you son of a bitch? A man who openly admits to killing five of my—" Nek caught himself. "Who admits to killing five men. But what the hell am I sitting here talking to you about it for? I don't know a goddamn thing about what you're talking about. All I know is you came here supposedly to talk about the Chiquita Silver Mine. Is that just bullshit, too—"

"That's right," cut in Hawker. "We came to talk about the mine. And here's what we have to say, so listen close. Ready? If you have your men release Jimmy Estes and Chuck Phillips within the next twenty-four hours, I promise not to destroy you and everything that has to do with your operation."

Nek shook his head slightly, as if he couldn't believe what he was hearing. "You really are out of your fucking tree, aren't you?" he said. "You got balls bigger than your brain. For one thing, I still got no idea what you're talking about. For another thing, if I did know what you were talking about, I'd be even more determined to make you look like the fucking fool you are." Nek held up one finger in exclamation. "Let me show you something, tough guy." He touched a switch on his desk, and three large mirrors in the room were illuminated. With the lights on, Hawker could see through the mirrors. Concealed behind each mirror, dimly seen, was a man holding an Uzi-size automatic weapon. All three of the weapons were pointed right at Hawker and Dulles.

Nek switched off the lights with a pleased expression on his face. "See?" he said, now clearly back in control. "I'm nobody's fool. Nobody's fool, *never*. You mentioned my three old partners. Well, what about them? You think I was afraid of them?" He snickered. "That's pure horseshit, 'cause they weren't worth my time then, and they sure as fuck ain't worth my time now. They've always been losers. Always. Always were. Always will be. Afraid of them? A man like me isn't afraid of gutter trash like them."

"Then why do you want their mine?"

Nek stiffened. "Because I'm a smart businessman, dumb shit. I've always been a smart businessman. That's why I'm a success and my three old partners are broken-down fools." He

67

waved toward the window. "Hell, out there I got me a jet that can fly me anywhere in the world I want. I got cars, women, racehorses, islands; shit, everything."

"You don't have your old friends," Hawker pressed. "And now you're afraid they're going to become as rich as you. That would be too bad, Nek, because it would show you up as the crook you are."

The old man slammed his hand on the chair and yanked open the drawer of his desk. "I'm not going to tell you where I'm keeping those bastards," he screamed, "and I'm not going to put up with any more of your bullshit!"

From the drawer the old man took a chrome-plated revolver, yanked the hammer back, and pointed the gun at Hawker's head.

EIGHT

Hawker and Dulles leaped at the old man simultaneously. Dulles got there first, just as the revolver exploded. His face was briefly contorted by the sound-impact, but the slug missed his head and rammed into the wall. He yanked the gun from Nek's hand and held it at the ready.

The vigilante was already rolling off the desk as the three mirrors ruptured and the bodyguards stepped through. He kicked at the light switch with his foot, and he breathed a sigh of relief when the room went black save for the light of the fire.

"Bastard! Motherfucker!" Bill Nek's voice was like the shriek of an hysterical woman.

There was the orange sputter of automatic weapons fire, and Hawker threw his body into a dark figure that stood before him. The impact snapped the bodyguard's head back to his spine, and he collapsed, unconscious.

Nek was screaming, "Stop firing, stop firing, you stupid shits! You'll hit *me!*"

The charcoal shapes of the bodyguards turned the barrels of their weapons toward the ceiling, frozen by Nek's orders and also by the knowledge that either Hawker or Dulles was probably armed by now.

"Tom? You okay?" Hawker shouted.

"Fine. I've got this revolver trained on Nek's head. I may just blow this crazy bugfucker all over the wall."

"Don't do it! Just keep him covered and move back toward me. Okay?"

The lanky form of Tom Dulles backpedaled into Hawker as the vigilante found the door handle, threw it open, then slammed it closed behind them as he pulled the Denver cop out into the hall.

Hawker flicked the safety tang of the Uzi onto full automatic and shot a quick burst through the door.

"That'll hold them a minute or two. Let's get the hell out of here," he shouted.

They were in the great hall of the house. There was the noise of heavy feet running in all directions, it seemed. Hawker crashed through a side entrance with Dulles right after him.

"What in the hell are we running for? We didn't do anything!"

"I don't want those Germans to get their hands on us," Hawker yelled back. "Have you ever been worked over by a professional? I don't recommend it. You piss blood for about a week."

Behind them, one of the doors swung open, and slugs cut through the tree limbs over their heads. Hawker turned and returned fire. "Shit," Dulles yelled, "if you kill one of those bastards, I'm going to be filling out forms for the next year!"

"I'm just keeping them honest," said Hawker. "They could have wasted us easily enough back in Nek's library. Nek is nuts. He really wanted to put a round through my brain. But those krauts are too smart. They know you're a cop. They don't want to get into anything too stinky."

Once again, slugs brought autumn leaves splattering to the ground like confetti. "For not trying to hit us, they're coming damn close!"

"They want to show us they can play rough." The vigilante turned and emptied the rest of the Uzi into the outside wall of the fortress. "But now they know we can play rough, too."

They were running through a park of trees and close-cropped grass. Ahead was the black wrought-iron gate. Dulles turned toward it, but Hawker shouted, "Hey, that thing's hot. If you get fried on their fence, they can just say you were trying to do a B & E. We've got to go back out the way we came."

"That guard was armed!"

"Yeah, but he cares about living and dying. People like that, you don't have much to fear from. He'll move. Skip a couple of rounds off the asphalt into the wall of the guardhouse. He'll get the idea. I'd use the Uzi, but it's empty."

They were sprinting now along a high copse. The stone guardhouse was less than fifty yards away. More men were behind them, running hard as Dulles snapped off two shots that pinged off the rock wall.

Hawker got a glimpse of the guard's shoes protruding from beneath the desk as he and Dulles flew by. The guard was hiding. And he didn't look up as the vigilante slammed the iron gate behind them.

"I'll drive," Hawker yelled, skidding to a halt beside Dulles's car. "Keep the revolver handy."

Hawker twisted the key, mashed the accelerator to the floor, and fought to control the car as they fishtailed onto the road and away from Bill Nek's secluded estate.

Ahead were the bright, blue-white snowy peaks of the Rockies, looming over the Denver skyline. The city made gray and silver concrete stalagmite shapes at the foot of the mountains.

"Holy shit," Tom Dulles exclaimed, releasing a great breath. "Is your life always this wild?"

"I'm usually home every night with a good book."

Dulles hooted. "You don't think I believe that shit, do you? Jesus, man, you've got balls made of grade-A granite! I can't believe you just bullshitted your way in to see the great William Nek, the richest man in Denver, and then sat there and told the old fart you would destroy his entire empire if he didn't cooperate. Jesus, did you see his face when you said it? I thought he was going to blow a tube in his brain. What a bluff you made!"

"I wasn't bluffing," Hawker said quietly. "I meant every word of it."

Dulles looked dubious. "Look, Hawk, I don't doubt you're damned good at what you do. I mean, I know firsthand how good you can be! But be realistic. How can you destroy Nek's whole empire?"

"Easily," Hawker replied. "Nek is a business. He's insane, but he's still a business. I can shake him up good on the outside, and I have an associate who's so rich that he could buy and sell Nek. Believe me, my friend could find a way to turn the screws so tight on the so-called Silver King that he would never recover. That's why I wanted to see Nek in person. It's damned serious business. And when you think about it, this whole case is kind of a long-term domestic squabble. Four old friends have a fight fifty years ago. Bad blood continues. One of them—Nek—goes a little crazy. He wants to show his old partners how powerful he's become, so he flexes some muscle." Hawker shrugged as he steered the car north toward the heart of Denver. "I wanted to give him a chance to drop it. I wanted to give him a chance to poke his hands in his pockets and go shuffling back to the others and ask for their forgiveness. A sane person would have accepted my offer. Don't think for a minute Nek really didn't recognize my name. I saw the look in his eyes. He's heard of me, heard of what my organization is capable of. But he's gone too screwy. And I think he's been screwy for a long time. I'll bet if we had a way of getting inside information, we'd find out that Nek has used kidnapping and murder and God knows what else to intimidate people before. He's got this weird, wild expression in his eyes. I've seen it before. I've seen it in the faces of psychopaths and kinks. That man has some screws loose, mark my words. He is a thoroughly dangerous man."

"How clever of you to notice," purred the voice of a stranger from the backseat. Hawker and Dulles both started as the precision *lick-click* of a revolver being cocked echoed in their ears. "Now, Mr. Hawker, if you are done philosophizing, kindly pull this car over to the curb before I am forced to shoot one of your ears off!"

It was the husky, lubricious voice of a woman. He could see a choice rectangle of her face in the mirror: silky platinum hair, rust-colored, auburn eyes, waspish pug nose, delicate cheekbones, lips rouged pink on a mouth that now wore a slightly cruel smile.

He felt the cool barrel of the snub-nosed .38 touch his earlobe.

The vigilante saw a gravel berm, and he pulled over.

"Now," said the woman easily, "I want Mr. Policeman to get out of the car."

"What?" Dulles's head pivoted to look at the woman. He smiled slightly when he saw how beautiful she was, but the smile vanished from his face when she leveled the revolver at his nose.

"Did I say you could turn around, Mr. Policeman?"

"Look, lady—"

"Nor did I give you permission to talk!" With his peripheral vision, Hawker saw her nudge Dulles's head with the revolver. "What I told you to do was to get out of the car. That's exactly what I expect you to do."

Dulles shook his head. "Lady, you are making one hell of a mistake. I don't know who you are or why you're doing this, but I swear to you—"

"And I swear to you, Mr. Policeman, that I will shoot you in an exceedingly uncomfortable spot if you do not obey me this instant!"

"You crazy broad—"

"Go ahead, Tom," Hawker interrupted firmly. "Take a walk. I'll try to make it back to the hotel by tonight—"

"No more talking!"

Tom Dulles reluctantly got out of the car and slammed the door. The vigilante saw the quick, studious look he gave the woman. Hawker knew the Denver cop was trying to memorize every detail of her face, eyes, and hair for future reference.

Hawker hoped Dulles would not have to use the information to try to pin a murder rap on her—his murder.

"Drive," commanded the woman.

"Drive where?"

"Just keep going straight until I tell you otherwise."

Hawker put the car in gear and began to drive. Behind them, Dulles grew smaller, then disappeared, still trudging along on foot.

Hawker could see the woman better in the rear-view mirror now that she had settled comfortably into the backseat. Her fashion-model face fulfilled the promise of startling beauty that his first quick look had given him. Her platinum hair fell like spun glass over her down vest and black ski sweater. She had the flavor of money about her. It was more than just the diamond earrings and the expensive gold watch that flashed in the mirror from time to time as she waved the revolver to illustrate directions. It was her presumptuous attitude of control. She was used to giving orders. She was used to getting her way. That she had taken him at gunpoint seemed not to disturb her in the least. It was almost as if they were going for a Sunday ride, or as if Hawker were a chauffeur. How old was she? Maybe twenty-two, maybe much older—it was hard to tell in the forgiving light of the car's interior. Who the hell was she?

"Turn left at the next corner," she called. "Keep going until you see Meeker Boulevard. Then turn right. Go about three miles. That'll take us to Interstate 70. Get on the westbound ramp and take us out of Denver."

Hawker looked in the mirror. "You're not taking me back to Nek so his goons can work me over?"

"What a ridiculous thing to say. Why would I take you back to my husband?"

"Husband?"

The woman gave a slow, sardonic laugh. "For once, I see surprise on the face of the great James Hawker. Such a cold, cold face you have, Mr. Hawker. But it's a strange kind of coldness. It's like—like cold fire." She seemed pleased by the description, and her voice began to purr. "Yes, that's it. Cold fire. But a rather handsome face in a brutal sort of way, with your autumn-colored hair and that crooked nose. I've heard a bit about you, Mr. Hawker. Oh, yes, quite a lot, really. Actually, I've read about you. My husband has been very worried that you would be coming. He's suspected for weeks. He had some of his people draft a report on you. Quite a report it was, too!"

"Mrs. Nek," Hawker said, "if you don't mind my asking, why are you doing this?"

"I'm getting to that, Mr. Hawker. Please don't be so impatient. We have quite a long ride ahead of us. I assure you, you will have all your questions answered if you cooperate with me. Actually, I was just getting to one of the important points. The report on you. I read it, or read most of it, anyway. I must admit to having been fascinated by what I read. Such an interesting man you are, Mr. Hawker. World traveler, world criminal, world playboy, world rogue. It seems everyone loves you and fears you at the same time. And what a record with the ladies!" She made a ticking sound with her tongue. "Yes, my husband's people always draft very thorough reports. I knew immediately that I had to meet you. There was no doubt in my mind that you were the man I needed to help me."

"Help you?" said Hawker. "Your husband just tried to kill me fifteen minutes ago. His men are still after me. If your husband knew we were together, he'd probably have us both tortured."

"Of course he would," the woman said. "Why else would I have gone to such extraordinary lengths to meet you? Several days ago I made arrangements with old Blake, our gatekeeper. I instructed him to notify me if you happened to arrive. I also told him that under no circumstances were you to drive in on your own. Your car was to be left outside the estate. Blake followed my orders perfectly, and I sequestered myself on the floor of your backseat, revolver in hand."

"But why, for Christ's sake?" Hawker exclaimed. "You're making absolutely no sense—"

"Because I had to talk to you," the woman snapped. "I had to get you alone, and I knew there was no other way for me to do it. I need you, James Hawker, and I couldn't let my husband know how much. I need you because you're the one man who can help me kill the son of a bitch."

"What?"

"That's right, I want the bastard dead. I heard you talking to your policeman friend. And you were correct in everything you said about William Nek. He is a psychopath. He is a bug. He's a kidnapper and murderer and much, much more—"

"And you married him," Hawker said, his voice rising over the shaking hatred of the woman's.

"That's right! I married him! But if you think I'm going to tell you why, or if you think I'm going to try to justify my reasons, you're wrong as hell," she retorted. "I don't need a confidant. I need a man. I need someone fast and tough and experienced in—this kind of thing." She leaned forward in her seat. "Don't worry, I'll pay you well. Money's one thing we'll never have to argue about. Never will you get so much for doing so little. Upon the successful completion of my husband's assassination, I will hand to you personally one hundred thousand dollars in cash. Along with the money I will also give you a key and a signed, notarized authorization to take the contents of a safety deposit box at the Canadian Bank on Grand Cayman Island. In the safety deposit box you will find nine bricks of ninety-four percent pure gold. The bricks each weigh five pounds. At today's prices, those bricks would be worth over a quarter of a million dollars."

"If you read my dossier, you know that I already have plenty of money. More money than I could ever use."

"A person can always use more money, Mr. Hawker. Always."

"And you could drive down into the slums of Denver and hire someone to do it for five hundred bucks. Why offer me over three hundred thousand?"

"Because I want it done professionally. I don't want to ever be suspected of having had a hand in it. With you, I could be sure that I would never be implicated. Besides, for that much money, I want more than just murder. I want something else from you."

"Oh?" Hawker looked in the rearview mirror as the woman settled back in her seat again.

"Don't look so surprised." She motioned with her hand. Hawker noticed that she still had not put the revolver away. "Turn left here. See that gravel drive that goes into the trees and up the mountain? Follow it."

"I'm getting a little tired of your holding that gun on me."

"You still haven't given me your answer, Mr. Hawker. You still haven't said you would help me."

"And you haven't told me everything you want from me, Mrs. Nek."

"Don't call me that," the woman said with an edge in her voice. "Please don't call me that ever again."

"Then what—"

"Call me Melissa."

"Okay, then, Melissa—"

"And I'll tell you the rest of what I want when we get inside the house. Okay? Please just be patient."

Within two hundred yards, the gravel drive twisted and turned its way up a ledge to a Swiss-style chalet built into the side of the hill beneath trees ablaze with autumn leaves. It was a house out of Hans Christian Andersen. It was a gingerbread house of earth colors and elaborate latticework. There were oculus windows, parapets, arched doorways, and bay windows that looked out onto what must have been one of the most spectacular views possible of the city of Denver.

The woman got out of the car, her whole spirit seemingly brightened by just being near the house. "Like it?" she asked, making an embracing gesture with her arms.

"Very pretty," said Hawker. "I like it very much." It was his first real look at the woman. In her black ski sweater and designer jeans, she could have been any one of a hundred thousand of Colorado's interchangeable ski bunny beauties. But there was something frail and wild about the pale skin of her perfect face, about the soft and shining platinum blond hair, about the glittering, haunted blue eyes. Her nervousness reminded Hawker of an expensive Thoroughbred, one that had been bred a little too finely and suffered its beauty through delicacy.

"It's mine," the woman said. "All mine. Bill Nek doesn't even know anything about it. This house is the only thing in this entire world that has ever been completely mine. I had it built with money that I damn well deserved and took for myself. I designed it myself, too."

"I like it," said Hawker. "But if we drove all the way out here just to see—"

"Come on," the woman said anxiously. "Hold your questions till we get inside. Then I'll tell you anything you want to know."

The vigilante followed her up the steps to the broad porch that overlooked the hot tub, the well-groomed Oriental garden, the fountain, and the bird feeders. Inside, the house was chilly from disuse, but a stone fireplace covered one entire wall.

"Could you get a fire going?" the woman asked. "I'll pour some wine, get the upstairs hot tub going, and the two of us can get to know each other better—"

"Why don't you just tell me what you want, Melissa?"

The woman looked hurt, then evasive, then a glossy expression of defiance came into her eyes that was touchingly childlike. "For all that money, Hawker, I do want something else from you. It's strictly business. Nothing personal; even so, it may sound like a strange request. I decided on you because you must be very, very good at—it, and I want someone who is very, very good at it."

"What the hell is 'it,' Melissa?"

The woman's voice softened with nervousness. She took a deep breath. "I want you to take me . . . I want you to show me— to make me feel good as a woman. I will pay you the money if you take care of my husband, and if you can help me to experience what it is like to enjoy being with a man in bed . . ."

NINE

The woman had offered him more than three hundred thousand dollars to kill her husband and to take her to bed. What could she do if he refused? Judging by the way she held the revolver, it looked as if she might shoot him.

Hawker shook his head wearily.

He had heard that the ski craze had brought some awfully weird people into Colorado.

In the space of just a few days, it seemed he had already met a fair portion of them.

Hawker sighed and began to crumple newspapers and lay on tinder and logs, constructing a fire. "Look, lady," he began, "I really don't want to get involved in all this—"

"But didn't you come to Denver to kill my husband? I'm not asking that much more, am I?" Her chin drooped slightly and her eyes became shy, puppy-size.

"I'm not an assassin, Melissa. I didn't come to Colorado as a killer, I came because there are some people here who need help. I can't accept an assignment to kill someone in cold blood. And as far as the other thing—"

"Don't you find me attractive?" said the young blond woman. She had taken off her down vest and shaken her hair down over her shoulders.

Hawker lighted the fire. "It's not that I don't find you attractive. You know it's not that. You know damn well how pretty you are—"

"Oh? And how would I know that? Bill Nek rarely lets me out of the house. When I do leave, it has to be with a chauffeur. All the chauffeurs are Bill's personal spies. It's like being a prisoner."

"But you must have been with men before you married Nek—"

"Never! Never once! He would never have stood for it. He's crazy, I'm telling you. When he wants something, he *has* to have it. And when he owns something, he has to own it completely. It was the same with me. I have no idea what other men think about me, because Bill Nek has had control over me since I was much younger. And I have no idea what it is like to be with other men in bed, because I've only been with that disgusting old creature. The things he makes me do are terrible. He makes me want to vomit. But he can't do anything to me because his—thing doesn't work. And he could never ever make me feel good, because the touch of his hands makes me cringe."

The woman made a face of passionate distaste that was somehow mixed with a pathetic wanting. "I used to think that

I would never want to be with a man. Ever. But in the last year or so, something inside me has begun to change. I began to imagine things—how it would feel, what it would be like. I'd fantasize about some man coming and taking me away to show me. But I knew that I couldn't let myself fall in love with the man. And I knew he couldn't be in love with me. It would be too painful because Nek would make our lives living hell. I knew that, if I found the right man, it would have to be handled as a business deal."

The woman took three slow steps closer to the vigilante. The fire was crackling now, and she looked frail and pretty and very young. "So now I'm offering you the deal, Mr. Hawker. True, I brought you here at the point of a gun. But I don't often get the chance to escape from Nek's prison for a day without one of his chauffeurs, so I couldn't take the chance of your just telling me to get lost. In fairness to me, though, you have to admit that I've been very open and honest since we got to my house. So now I want your answer. Is it yes or is it no?"

The vigilante took a deep breath. The woman saw the negative expression on his face and said quickly, "You can't be expected to make up your mind until you've seen what you're getting. How thoughtless of me." In a reluctant gesture of touching uncertainty, Melissa Nek pulled the black ski sweater over her head and shook her silver hair back into place. "I'm not big," she said, "but I've kept myself in good shape. Don't you think?"

Hawker stood looking at one of the most perfect female bodies he had ever seen. She had small, full upturned breasts with long, pale pink nipples. The accent of her ribs disappeared smoothly in the tight swell of her jeans. "I'll take off my pants now, too, if you like—"

Hawker reached out and took her by the hand and pulled her to him. "You're trembling," he said quietly.

"It's—it's cold."

"Why don't you just admit that you're afraid, Melissa? There's nothing wrong with being afraid."

"Because I'm not afraid. This is just a sort of business transaction. You're being well-paid. You're a teacher, nothing more. Why should I be afraid of a teacher in my own employ?"

Hawker held the shivering woman close to him, feeling sorry for this strange beauty who had been crippled by a man who, more and more, seemed like a monster. "I haven't accepted your offer yet."

The woman tried to pull away from him. "Is it because I'm not pretty enough? I know you must have had many women a lot prettier than I—"

"You're beautiful," Hawker said. "You really are. But I'm not a paid assassin. I can't accept money for killing Bill Nek. I'll try to help you get away from him, though. I'll do anything I can to help you."

"And the other thing?" the woman asked in a small voice. "What about the other part of our business deal?"

The vigilante laughed. "I don't accept money for doing that, either."

"Then you won't help me?"

Hawker nuzzled his face into the woman's silk-soft hair. "If you have a swimsuit around this doll house of yours, go put it on. I'll meet you in the hot tub. We'll discuss it there."

"And wine? Can we have wine?"

The vigilante nodded. "You can have all the wine you want. But first, please put that damned gun away. You're beginning to make me nervous."

The indoor hot tub was on the exercise patio. There was a sauna, a steam room, an ice-water plunge pool, an exercise bar, and mirrors. The patio provided another fantasy view of Denver and the foothills of the Colorado Rockies. It was after five P.M., and the Mile High City was getting a misty autumn late-afternoon look.

Hawker stood leaning against the rail looking out when he heard the door behind him whoosh open.

The woman carried a bottle of champagne in one hand and two glasses in the other. The swimsuit she wore was really a sheer gray body stocking through which the outlines of her lithe body were traced in silver. Her legs were long and trim, and a bit of pale body hair escaped from the crotch seam.

"Did you bring a suit for me?" Hawker asked.

"Don't be silly. What would I be doing with a man's swimsuit? I'm afraid you'll just have to improvise. Do you want to open the champagne, or shall I?" A chill mountain wind swept across the porch, and the woman shivered slightly. Hawker took the magnum and the glasses. He nodded toward the bubbling, boiling, steaming hot tub. "Why don't you get in there before you catch cold?"

"But I thought I would take a steam first—"

"Hot tub first," he insisted. "The sun will be going down soon. We can sit and watch it and enjoy the wine."

The woman smiled, relaxing a little. "Like going to the theater, huh?"

"In Key West, they have toasts and applaud the sunset. It would be nice if you had a stereo—"

"I have a full Boise system! Everything built into the walls, the very best money can buy."

"I should have known. Poor little rich girl."

"What kind of music do you like?"

Hawker thought for a moment, actually enjoying himself. The woman might be a little crazy, but the idea of sitting in a hot tub and watching the sun set while listening to good music was attractive enough to make him forget the craziness of his day. "Sunset in the Rockies demands something kind of grand and instrumental, doesn't it? I don't suppose you have Copland's *Fanfare for the Common Man*, do you?"

The woman snapped her fingers. "That's the one they play a lot in the movies when the stagecoaches are headed across the prairie, right? The one with all the brass and timpani."

"I'm surprised you know it. But do you have it?"

She nodded. "I had my entire collection duplicated and brought out here—something like five thousand albums. It should be around someplace. It may take me awhile to find it—"

"It'll give me time to pour the wine and find a swimsuit."

"Such modesty!" The woman went swishing off, firm buttocks wagging, fingers finding the rim of her tights and pulling them down—the self-conscious action of a teen-age girl.

Christ, thought Hawker, as she disappeared into the house. How old can she be? Absolutely no older than twenty-seven, but probably closer to twenty-four. What kind of weird bastard is this Bill Nek to force a beautiful young creature like that to marry him? And what kind of parents could the girl have to let her go through with such a monstrous deal?

Hawker shook his head as he stripped off his shirt and slacks and unbuckled the empty holster and knife scabbard attached to his calves. It was only then that he remembered that Nek's goons still had his handgun and his Randall knife. The handgun he didn't care about. He had plenty of weaponry available. He was prepared for anything this mission to Colorado might demand. But he hated like hell to lose his Randall survival knife. It had been made especially for him by old Bo Randall of Orlando, Florida, one of the world's great knifemakers and a great American as well.

Hawker made a mental note to get the knife back if he ever found himself back inside Bill Nek's complex.

He had a feeling he would sometime soon.

Wearing only his beige jockey shorts, Hawker found the timer knobs on the sauna room and the steam room and switched them both on high. If the woman had only had Bill Nek as a lover, then she might demand a great deal of thawing before he could give her any pleasure.

He opened the champagne and watched the cork disappear over the precipice, arching toward Denver. He poured two glasses of the golden liquid, then stepped into the hot tub, feeling his scrotum contract upon contact with the steaming water.

From some unseen speakers came the first tentative trumpet calls of a symphony orchestra. At first it was too loud, then too soft, then the music was just loud enough to blend in with the sound of the wind as it filtered down off the mountaintop, through the trees.

Hawker took a sip of his champagne, made a face, and sighed. He would have preferred beer. He would have preferred to be with a woman he knew and liked. He would have preferred not to be in Colorado on a mission. But life, he knew, rarely deals out things that are preferred. The trick, he had learned, was not to expect the preferred deal, but to prefer the deal you happened to get.

All considered, things could have been a lot worse.

Melissa came wagging through the door, her left hand brushing nervously at her hair. The sun was growing gold and low over the mountains, and the pearly light showed goosebumps on her legs and the large erect eyes of her nipples beneath the thin silver fabric of the body stocking.

"Getting cold out," Hawker said. He patted the water. "Better get in."

"Are you—did you—are all of your clothes off?" She was peering down into the water, suddenly looking like a child afraid of snakes.

Hawker laughed. "Don't worry so much, Melissa. I'm wearing good American-made underwear. They'd pass for a swimsuit just about anyplace."

The woman touched her toe to the water experimentally. Hawker said, "You're having second thoughts, aren't you? You think that because you came on so strong, so businesslike, I'm going to feel obligated to ravish you. Well, I'm not. Frankly, I'd be just as happy if we skipped the sex part and just had a nice long talk. There's a lot I'd like to know about your husband—"

"I won't talk about Bill Nek," she interrupted firmly.

"Then we can talk about you," Hawker continued. "The point is, you don't have to do anything you don't want to do. And I'm sure as hell not going to do anything I don't want to do." He raised the glass to her. "Here, take your wine. Get in here before you freeze."

Melissa took a sip of the wine, shivered, then slid into the water. "Hoo! This feels good!" She was grinning.

Hawker reached out and touched his glass to hers. "To the relaxation of a beautiful woman."

"To my relaxation," Melissa said, looking at him over the rim of the glass, then stretching her arms back and sliding her foot over to rest on the vigilante's.

TEN

Hawker spent a heart-pounding hour going from the hot tub to the icy water of the plunge pool, then to the sauna, then to the steam room, then back to the plunge pool, then once again to the hot tub.

He began to wonder if his body would ever need to sweat again.

They kept sipping at the wine, kept drifting off into the reverie of music that matched the silver-tanged afterglow of sunset in the mountains, kept exchanging easy conversation. Hawker was aware that the woman was yawning more, stretching more, allowing more eye and body contact. He knew that she was coming around and would soon be ready to bed. The trick would be for him to keep from passing out before the time came.

"Steam room time!" Melissa called gaily, pouring the last few drops from the empty champagne bottle. She looked at the bottle with a pouting expression, then looked at Hawker. It was their second bottle, and she obviously wanted more.

"Hit the cold water, then the steam room. I'll get another bottle and meet you in there," Hawker said.

The vigilante walked barefoot and wet, his feet slapping, into the house. The fire was burning low, and he added more wood. In the kitchen, he found another magnum of wine, and a single lone Coors for himself. Seeing a beer in this house of expensive furnishings and in-crowd gismos was like seeing an old friend. He stopped in the bathroom, urinated, and noticed a bottle of coconut oil on the shelf. He took it outside with him.

Melissa was stretched out on the top deck of the cedar-wood-and-rock steam room. Her hands were locked behind her head so that the bone structure of her hips and pelvis was arched toward the ceiling. She opened one eye briefly as Hawker came in. "Umm, where's the wine?"

"Outside in the plunge pool chilling. Why do you keep that thing so cold? One more trip to that place, and my scrotum may just crawl to cover and decide not to come back out."

"It's good for your skin. It closes the pores, silly."

"I found something here that's supposed to be good for the skin, too." The vigilante held up the bottle of oil for inspection. "Care for a backrub, lady?"

"I'm not sure, James," she said in a small voice. "This has been so much fun, and now if you touch me and I can't make myself like it, it would spoil—"

"Nothing is going to be spoiled," Hawker" said, "and I don't want you to make yourself do anything. Just lie there. If you don't like it, tell me to stop. That's all there is to it. Okay?"

The woman took a deep breath. "Okay, dear. But I'm warning you, this is a first for me. I know hardly anything about—about loving a man."

Hawker opened the coconut oil, poured some into his hand, and smeared it on her legs. He began to massage the oil into her skin, enjoying the scent of it, enjoying the sleepy, faraway look on the woman's perfect face.

As he rubbed her legs and the bare skin of her neck and shoulders, he let his fingers stray, brushing her inner thigh, delicately touching her breasts, grazing her pubis with an extended thumb.

"Umm," she moaned. "Umm, yes." Her face was flushed, beaded with the hot steam, and she did not resist when Hawker slid his hands into the shoulders of her body stocking, then stripped the soaking garment down over her chest, stomach, and thighs, then tossed it aside.

He poured the coconut oil over her entire front. His hands slid up and down her body, massaging her as she lifted, arched, moaned, and cried. Her breasts became milk-white projectiles, projectiles so pale that blue veins formed a throbbing network of color beneath the fine skin, and her pink nipples swelled as if to explode. Her head was thrown back, eyes closed, mouth open, tongue tracing her full lips. Hawker bent and kissed her. She tensed for a moment, then her small hand wound itself in his hair, and she pulled his mouth hard against hers.

"I've never felt like this, never ever felt like this," she moaned. Hawker kissed her again and moved his left hand down her body to the inside of her thigh, stroking the hot clitoral swell beneath her silken pubic hair. She made a low growling shudder, a gurgling zoo sound that fit the primal atmosphere of the steam room. She was breathing so heavily that Hawker feared for a moment that she might be having some kind of attack. It must have been 120 degrees in that steam room! He took his hands from her and attempted to lift her to her feet, but she pressed his hand back to her vagina with a feral quickness. "Don't stop," she groaned. "Not now— not ever . . ."

Her hands began to search his body, then began to slide up and down his lean stomach and heavily muscled thighs, then slid his underwear down, and the vigilante stepped out of them.

Melissa was on her back, her head craned backward, looking at Hawker, who stood above her. She took him in her two small hands, touching him gently, studying him carefully as if she had never seen a fully developed man before. Then with a hungry, almost feverish lunge, she took him into her mouth. She was like a starving, wild creature, her tongue hot and alive as she cupped his buttocks in her two hands and plunged him deeply into her mouth, again and again.

Finally, Hawker had to pull away. "I'm dizzy as hell with this heat," he said. "Let's go outside—"

"No! Here—please, here. I've never felt so wonderful, so alive in my life! James, I'm scared if I leave now this feeling will never come again!"

The vigilante made a fluttering noise of resignation with his lips as the woman found him once again with her hungry hands, spread her legs so wide that it seemed she wanted to swallow his entire body, then steered him into her with a sharp hip thrust and a yip of pain, then pleasure.

"This feeling will come again," muttered Hawker, "but I'm not sure I will . . ."

After all the firelights he had been in, all the wars, the shootouts, the knife fights, fistfights, and mortal grudge matches, it crossed James Hawker's mind how ironic it would be to die of heart failure in a steambath with the lips of a shockingly beautiful twenty-five-year-old virgin gridlocked on his tallywhacker.

"Melissa, I've got to get out of here before I faint! I'll give you another chance. Damn it, let go!"

The vigilante went crashing through the door into the cold, clear wind of the Rocky Mountain night. Below, the lights of Denver glittered and glimmered with all the promise of autumn. Hawker took a quick look at himself in one of the full-length mirrors. "Jesus, I lost so much weight in there I look like Wally Cox," he panted.

"It still looks perfect to me," said the woman as she filed exuberantly out behind him. "God, I had no idea anything could feel so good. It feels wonderful! Delicious! You taste delicious!" She took Hawker by the arm, but he pulled away and, with a moment's hesitation, dropped himself into the icy water of the plunge pool.

Shit!

"Isn't it the best, most wonderful, greatest thing you've ever felt! No wonder that old bastard Bill Nek promised to geld any man who touched me. He knew that if I ever found out how much fun it is with a healthy man, he would never ever get me back!"

Hawker got out of the pool and brushed the water from his

close-cropped dark red hair. What the icy water hadn't done to discourage his libido, the revelation about gelding had. "Yes, Melissa, it feels wonderful and nice and all of those things you said. But don't you think you ought to prove to yourself that you can enjoy it in places other than a steam room? Christ, I feel like corned beef."

Standing naked, sweating, her entire body flushed by heat and lovemaking, Melissa Nek was a truly beautiful specimen, as wild-looking and tawny as a lioness. "Yes!" she shouted to the night. "In the bedroom, the living room, the kitchen, in front of the fire—"

"You're asking a lot for only three hundred thousand," Hawker said, climbing from the cold water.

The woman looked at him, then did a double take. "My god, what happened? You're all shriveled!"

"It's not shriveled, it's camouflaged. He's down there some-place hiding."

"How about if I yell 'fire,' then grab him when he jumps out?" the woman said, only half-kidding. She stroked Hawker's inner thigh and took him into her hand. "The poor darling. I know just the thing to get him back out. Come with me."

Being led toward the house by his exhausted member, the vigilante said, "Okay—but only if I can finish my beer first."

Later that evening, they lay wrapped in each other's arms naked by the fire. The vigilante stirred, opened one eye, and peeked at his watch.

Ten eighteen P.M.

"Hey," he whispered. "Hey, you."

The woman yawned, scratched, smiled. "Hey, yourself," she purred. "Are you rested up? Do you want to do it again?"

"We don't want to overdo it," Hawker said quickly, "what with you being a beginner and all. Besides, I have to be going. When you hijacked me this afternoon, we took my friend's car. Right now, he's probably wondering if I'm dead or alive." Hawker glanced down and added wryly, "Frankly, I'm not sure myself."

He stood. "Come on, I'm going to have to drop you near your house. I'll bet Nek's having fits."

The woman stretched luxuriously. "I have a Porsche down in the garage. I bought it just in case something like this ever came up. If the old bastard asks me where I've been, I'll tell him I got restless and went out and bought a car."

"Clever," said Hawker. "What husband wouldn't fall for that?"

She wrapped her arms around his waist tenderly. "I'm going to see you again, aren't I, James? I don't think I could bear not to see you again. Besides, we have a business deal, don't we?"

"I'm not an assassin, Melissa. I'm not going to take a contract to murder your husband."

"But you've already fulfilled the other half of the bargain. You made me feel so wonderful tonight, James. I've never felt so good in my life."

Hawker kissed the woman tenderly on the forehead. He was beginning to feel an unexpected affection for this troubled, impulsive, and spoiled woman. "There is something you can do for me, Melissa. I don't need money, and even if I did I couldn't take any for this. But there is something you can do."

She rubbed her cheek against his chest. "Anything, darling. Just name it."

"Your husband—Bill Nek—is holding two men prisoner someplace in the mountains. They were being held in an abandoned silver mine, but that may have changed. Anyway, I need to find out where they are, Melissa. It's very important. Is there any chance you could find out the location?"

The woman stepped back, thinking. "He keeps all his private papers locked and guarded. In his office, though, there are a lot of maps of Colorado. Those aren't locked. If I could sneak in there and get a look, they might tell me something. He's always scribbling on maps."

"Just as long as you don't get caught. I'd feel like hell if you got into trouble trying to help me."

She kissed him quickly. "I'd do anything for you, darling. Anything in the world. But only if you promise that this won't be our last time. Promise me?"

Hawker was putting on his clothes. "I have a rule about making promises to women. It's something I never do—not since I said yes to my ex-wife, anyway."

"Ah, the bitter divorced man."

"Not bitter at all. I married a very nice woman. It was a mistake, and we both realized it, and we split. She now lives with a bisexual fashion designer, and they're both very busy with a political action group demanding a cure for AIDS. I wish them both well. I still send her a card on her birthday."

"Then why do you sound just a little bitter?"

"Well, maybe just a little. But I'm still not going to make you any promises."

Hawker found a pad and pencil by the phone, wrote her unlisted number down and put it in his pocket, then wrote the telephone number of his hotel room (but not the number of his hotel room) on another slip of paper and handed it to her. "If you learn anything, give me a call. Is there any way I can reach you at Nek's house?"

She shook her head. "I have a private room, in fact, a private wing of the house. And that includes a great many telephones and three private numbers, but I'm sure that old bastard has them all tapped. He's a fanatic for security. When I get back, he'll practically have me interrogated by those Nazis he keeps around the place. He hates it when I sneak out alone."

"Tell him you bought the Porsche as a surprise for him," Hawker suggested. "That will explain your secrecy."

The woman's eyes flashed. "I wouldn't buy that evil, evil creature anything. Ever. He knows that—"

"Then why does he keep you if you hate him so?"

The woman's face lost its flush of pleasure, and Hawker was immediately sorry that he had asked. "He keeps me because he sees me as his piece of property. That's why; He makes me do things. Terrible things. What we did tonight, you and me, it was good, it was clean, it was a strong, pure thing we did. But the things Nek makes me do are sick. They're nauseating. I know that he watches me when I'm there in the nasty house. I know he has ways of seeing me when I'm in the shower or the bath or on the toilet. Two-way mirrors, maybe. Or some kind of video setup. I can almost feel his nasty eyes on me. I can feel him touching me with his eyes—and there's not a thing in the world I can do about it!" Hawker wrapped his arm around the woman as her voice broke and she began to cry.

"There is something you can do about it, Melissa," he said softly. "It's called divorce. This is no longer the Old West. Nek may be the richest man in Denver, but he doesn't make the laws. Get a lawyer and have the courts protect you. Sell this house and use the money to move to Europe. You have a lot of options."

"You don't understand, you don't understand," she wailed miserably. "My life is so awful, and there's nothing I can do to change it. Nothing!"

Hawker tried to make her feel better, but she could not be comforted.

Melissa Nek was still sobbing as Hawker stepped out into the Colorado night and drove back down the mountain to Denver.

ELEVEN

The telephone rang at five minutes after two in the morning. Hawker's hand speared out, slapped the end table a few times, and found the receiver.

"James? God, where have you been? I've been calling you all night."

It was a woman's voice. A good, husky, firm voice. He was so sleepy, his mind first registered the voice as Melissa's. But then he realized he was mistaken. "Lomela? What is it? Is something wrong?" Hawker sat up in bed and found the light.

It took him another moment to realize that he was in his Denver hotel room—a suite, really. Deep pile carpet, tasteful wallpaper, kitchenette with a microwave and wet bar, artificial fireplace, mini-health spa in place of a bathroom, his clothes mounted on fiber hangers in the open closet, his weaponry sealed in two coffin-size packing crates, both padlocked.

"I called Tom Dulles this afternoon," Lomela said. "He said you were in some kind of trouble. He was real upset, and Tom doesn't upset easily. He was damned worried about

you, James, but he wouldn't tell me much about it. He said
he would get back to me as soon as he knew anything. But
then the phone went out in this cabin where we're staying. It
snowed up here in our part of the range late this afternoon,
and I guess some tree limbs couldn't take it and they fell and
knocked the telephone wires down. God, I've been frantic all
night. I just got up to make sure the kids were doing okay, and
I tried the phone. Wonder of wonders, it worked."

"How are the kids, Lomela? Are they settling down after
what happened to them?"

The woman laughed easily. "James, I wish I had the recov-
ery powers them kids have. Acted like nothing in the world happened to 'em. Kidnappers don't mean nothing to those two. Some
kids have cast-iron stomachs. Mine must have cast-iron nerves."

"Good." Hawker smiled. "I was worried about them."

"And I was worried about you," Lomela replied. "Can't you
tell me about it, James? Did it have something to do with trying to find those men you're after?"

"In a way, Lomela. But there's nothing to worry about now.
I'm fine. Promise."

Her voice became shy. "You think there's any chance of you
maybe sneaking up here tomorrow to sort of say hello? I sure
did enjoy our little visit together. I promise you won't be disappointed if you come see me. In fact, I'll make sure you get
everything you want. Everything and more, James, honey."

The vigilante patted his stomach. He felt the way he once
had as a kid when he had eaten too many olives. "I'd love to,
Lomela," he said, trying to sound enthusiastic. "But I think
Tom already has something planned for us."

"I bet it has something to do with my daddy taking a gun and going up into those mountains to look for Jimmy Estes and Mr. Phillips, doesn't it?"

Hawker sat up straighter. "Your father did what?"

"Well, you only met Daddy that one time, but he's got a real stubborn streak in him. He got real restless staying up here in this here cabin. He said he was tired of hiding. So this morning he just up and took his Winchester, some supplies, and that nasty old pack mule of his and headed out. He said nobody in the state knows more about abandoned silver mines than he does, so he figured he'd try to flush them out. I made him promise to come back and tell you or Tom, though, once he finds them."

"Didn't you try to stop him, Lomela?"

"God knows, I did. But he's such a jar-headed old fool. Got to stewing over the idea of an Easterner—you—having to come in to help us with a Colorado problem. Made him real mad, it did. I tried everything to talk him into staying, but it was no use. When that old man makes up his mind to do something, he does it. It worries me, him being out in that snowstorm."

"We need to find him, Lomela. He's going to get himself into trouble out there. And I can't help him if I don't know where he is."

"I can't go out looking, James. I've got the babies. Besides, I promised Tom I wouldn't leave the cabin."

Hawker looked at his watch. "How long would it take me to get up there? An hour, maybe?"

"Don't even think about coming up now. What could you

do in the dark? You don't know these mountains. My daddy will be fine until morning at least. Remember, he's spent almost his whole life hiking these Rockies. He knows how to camp, and where, even at his age."

"Then I'll talk to Tom, and we'll come up tomorrow, okay?"

"I'd rather you come up by yourself, James," Lomela said in a flirtatious voice. "That way, maybe we could slip off for a bit and—"

The vigilante was laughing. "If we're going to slip off, woman, you're going to need some sleep. God knows I am."

"I'll be waiting, James."

Hawker switched off the light.

Next time I come to Colorado, he thought, I'm going to bring some vitamins.

The cold front that had brought snow to the mountains slid down into Denver during the night. Hawker had double rashers of bacon, toast, and four poached eggs in the hotel restaurant. His table was by a window. As pedestrians strolled by, their breath vaporized.

He went back up to his room to get the goose-down vest that seemed to be more a Colorado state uniform than it did a piece of clothing.

Just as he was about to pull the door shut behind him, the telephone rang.

"Hello?"

"Mr. James, I'm so glad I caught you. I decided I would like to have that oil painting framed for my husband. You're quite right. It would make a very nice Christmas present."

Even though it was subdued in a cool, business-like tone, the voice of Melissa Nek was immediately recognizable. Hawker played along without hesitation.

"I think you're making a wise decision, Mrs. Nek. How can I help you?"

"Well, you can either send a boy out to our estate to pick up the painting, or I can drop it off in town this afternoon. I'll be coming in around one."

"Perhaps we could meet for lunch," Hawker suggested. "That would give us more time to discuss exactly what you want."

"A very good idea," the woman replied. "Shall we meet at Marseille? I remember you saying you liked French food."

"Marseille would be fine," said the vigilante, who detested French food even more than he disliked the French citizenry.

"One P.M.," said the woman. "And remember, not a word to my husband's business associates. This is to be a surprise."

Hawker hung up, feeling as if his luck were about to change. The oil painting Melissa had mentioned would undoubtedly be a map. Could she really have found the right map, the one showing the place where the two kidnapped men were being kept?

Hawker felt a small charge of adrenaline move through him.

This was exactly the break he had been needing. He had been on the defensive ever since he had arrived in Colorado. He had been reacting, not acting.

He longed for a chance to take the offensive against Nek and his henchmen. The more he saw of the Silver King and his operation, the more he was struck by the putrescent spirit that marked it. Everything Nek and his men touched seemed dirtier for it, sickened by it.

Hawker thought about Melissa Nek for a moment with a fondness that startled him. An odd woman, no doubt. But then, she had lived an odd life.

At an early age, she had somehow fallen under Nek's power. He had forced her to marry him, and then he had abused her physically. The things he made Melissa do had so disgusted her that she refused to even talk about them.

Many women would have been forever dwarfed by such maltreatment, forever sickened and bitter toward men.

But Melissa's good instincts had somehow survived. Something deep inside her had insisted that she try to live, try to experiment with life.

Hawker had been her first experiment. And it had been a success. Now she was out to help him, do a favor in return.

The vigilante just hoped she wasn't caught. Bill Nek wasn't the type to show much mercy, and the loss of Melissa would be a hell of a loss.

He hoped she took care.

One thing her call did was change his plans for the entire morning. He had planned to meet Tom Dulles and head up into the mountains to look for Robert Carthay. Carthay was taking a hell of a chance looking for Nek's hitmen on his own, and he had to be stopped.

But now Dulles would have to try to find and stop the old man on his own.

Hawker called the Denver cop and told him that he wouldn't be able to make it. Dulles wasn't convinced he was making a wise choice.

"Hell, Hawk, that woman's crazy! She's the one who stuck

a gun to our heads and kidnapped us. When you think about it, it's damned embarrassing to have been handled like that by a woman—"

"I agree that she's no ordinary woman," the vigilante put in. "But I think she really may have something for us."

"Leading you into a trap is more like it."

"If that's so, she could have nailed me last night. She had plenty of opportunity to slip away and get in touch with her husband."

"That's another thing that bothers me," Dulles objected. "I've lived in Colorado all my life, and I've known about Bill Nek most of that time. You know, a man that rich gets all sorts of stories told about him. But I hardly ever heard anything about his wife. I mean, *nothing*. After she drove off with you yesterday, it started to bother me. I mean, these ugly old rich dudes like to buy themselves beautiful rich socialites. Then they like to show them off at parties and charity balls, stuff like that. Nek is as rich and ugly as a man can get, so he should have a beautiful socialite wife, right?"

"She is beautiful," Hawker put in.

"Yeah, but she never gets out. Hell, I didn't even remember hearing about the wedding. So last night, while I was fuming around wondering if you were dead or alive, I went down to the *Denver Post* offices. A friend of mine works in the library there. The 'library' is now what newspapers used to call the morgue—"

"Only a lot more computers," Hawker added.

"Right. So I looked up Nek. And you know what?"

"They hardly had a damned thing on him."

"Right," said Dulles. "All these years he's lived in Denver, and all they had was a few anonymous milquetoast stories on Nek as a silver pioneer, as a minor contributor to some local civic projects. Stuff like that. He's made the Fortune 500 list every year, but the local reporters can't even get him to make a comment about it. He's such a recluse that people hardly even notice that he is a recluse."

"Was there anything about Melissa?"

"One tiny little story," Dulles said. "It was in the Sunday feature section. The story was all of two inches long. It was just a blurb that said that Nek, known as the Silver King, had been married to an eighteen-year-old girl named Melissa Agno."

"Agno? What the hell kind of name is that?"

"Story didn't say. You could tell the reporter had taken the information straight from county records. Tried to flesh it out with some background on Nek, but there wasn't a thing on the woman. Hell, it didn't even appear in the paper until about a month after their wedding."

"How long ago was that?"

"Just over five years ago. Since then, there hasn't been one mention of Mrs. William Nek in *The Denver Post*."

"Was Nek ever married before?"

"According to the story—and I wouldn't put much faith in that—it was the first marriage for both of them. But there was a rumor around that Nek had a live-in maid for a lot of years."

"Oh? Do you know anything about her?"

"Not a thing. I guess live-in maids aren't all that uncommon," said Dulles.

"But when a sixty-nine-year-old multimillionaire marries

an eighteen-year-old girl, you'd think it would get more notice from the press."

"Hell"—Dulles laughed—"that kind of story went out in this state with stories about interracial marriages and sex-change operations."

"You've got some real weird folks living here in Colorado," Hawker said dryly.

"Yeah, and most of them are from someplace else. If you want to see the real weirdos, go to Aspen and hang around the Hotel Jerome for a while. They ought to put a tent over that place and charge admission. Real Coloradoans won't go anywhere near it."

"Well, let's hope Nek's wife really does have some information we can use," said Hawker.

"If she does know the location of the place where they're keeping Jimmy Estes and Chuck Phillips, what are you going to do?" Dulles asked.

"I like you, Tom," said the vigilante, smiling, "so I'm going to do you a favor. I'm not going to tell you what I'm going to do."

TWELVE

The waiter was a typical French waiter. He was surly and inefficient. The food was typically French food. It was complicated, the portions were small, and it was ridiculously overpriced. The atmosphere of the restaurant was typically French. It was small, dirty, and badly ventilated.

Hawker and Melissa Nek sat at a dark corner table studying a U.S. Geological Survey map. The woman wore a chic, slinky gray dress and a hat that looked to be out of a 1940s movie. The clothes made her look older—they gave her a Rita Hayworth sultriness.

"Are you sure he's not going to miss this?" Hawker asked her for the fourth time.

"I told you that I'm not sure about anything," the woman replied. "He told me he was going to be away from the house for a few days. He was still really mad about you and the policeman making him look like a fool. He had a real dangerous look in his eye when he left this morning."

"That's what I'm worried about," said Hawker. "I don't want him to take it out on you."

"He already had his chance this morning. When I came back with the new car, he acted like he couldn't care less. He's very preoccupied about something."

"Yeah," said Hawker. "He's afraid his old partners are going to make a success out of the Chiquita Silver Mine. He's afraid they'll prove that they're as good as he is. That's why he wants the mine so badly. He has a screw loose."

"Don't tell me!" The woman snorted. "I live with him."

The vigilante thought for a moment, then spoke. "Melissa, I know you don't like to talk about it, but I really would like to know the history of you and Nek. I don't know anything about how you came to marry him, and maybe I can help—"

The blonde touched her index finger to his lips, silencing him. "You've already helped, James," she said softly. "You've helped more than you can ever know." Beneath the table, she nudged her toe up under Hawker's slacks and massaged his calf as she added, "It hurts me to talk about it. I know that's hard for you to understand. But when I'm with you, all the craziness of my life disappears. It almost seems as if it never happened. That's why I don't want to talk about it. When I talk about it, it makes the nice fantasy of you disappear." She reached across the table and brushed the back of her hand on his cheek. "Let me keep my fantasy, okay? Help me not to spoil it. Don't ask me anymore, okay?"

"Okay, Melissa. But if you ever need help, a different kind of help—"

111

"Quit, please," she said, her voice husky. "You make me so damned emotional. Come on, look at the map and tell me what you think."

The map was a relief map of the Colorado Rockies. Even on paper the mountains were spectacular. The vigilante noticed several circles penciled in around small mountain towns like Leadville, Redcliff, Silverthorne, Marble, and Ragged Mountain. Beside the circles were scribbled numbers in odd sequence.

"What do the numbers mean?" Hawker asked.

The woman shrugged. "I've thought a lot about it, and I still don't know for sure. It probably has something to do with his lease dates and expiration dates. The rest of the numbers probably refer to the various claims he's filed, maybe, or the dates when he filed.

"Yeah," said Hawker. "I can see that now. Most of these claims are really old."

"They would have to be," said Melissa. "They're in the White River National Forest area. They don't allow mining claims there anymore. See, that's half the key to the old bastard's success. He filed so many claims before there were any regulations that he's grandfather-claused in on places where no one else is allowed to operate."

"These aren't the only claims he has in the state, though, are they?" Hawker asked.

"No way. He has hundreds and hundreds. I imagine he has active and abandoned silver mines in almost every county of Colorado."

"Then why did you bring just this map?"

"Because I overheard him talking to the pilot of his Learjet on the phone. He was telling him to make arrangements to fly to Aspen this morning. These are the mines closest to the Aspen airport."

The vigilante smiled. "Good work, woman. I may just have to hire you."

"Come on," she blushed. "You always work alone. Your dossier says so."

"Not always." Hawker laughed.

"Does that mean I can come with you when you leave for Aspen?"

"How do you know I'm going to rush right up to Aspen?"

"Because I know you," said the woman. "And I know how anxious you are to help your friends rid themselves of this whole business. My guess is you'll leave for Aspen the moment we finish our lunch."

Hawker looked at the dollop of strained potatoes on his plate and the coin-size circle of beef hidden behind a dirty sprig of parsley. The French, he thought as he poked at the untouched lunch, are the spoiled brats of Western civilization. Because they are lazy and because they are cowards, they are the eternal prey of would-be dictators. When other nations rush to their rescue, the French unfailingly end up hating their rescuers more than their conquerors. To a gullible world, only the French sense of snobbery keeps them from joining the ranks of the pathetic.

Hawker touched his tongue to the beef, then returned the beef to his plate. "You are wrong," he said. "My lunch was finished before the waiter came. I'm going to leave for Aspen now. Can I take this map?"

The woman smiled. "As long as you promise to bring it back to me."

"I promise," said the vigilante, patting the woman's hand. "I'll be back before you know it."

The vigilante returned to his hotel and made two quick calls. One was to Jacob Montgomery Hayes in Chicago. The other was to Hayes's acid-witted butler, Halton Collier Hendricks. Hendricks was in the west of Ireland, taking the "sea cure," as he put it, for a case of the "American doldrums."

Hawker respected these two men more than anyone else in the world, and he had a nice long talk with both of them. Mostly, though, he let them know what he had planned. In the event he wasn't successful, he didn't want to leave without saying good-bye to his two old friends.

That day would come, of course. He lived a life of concentrated violence, of unnatural violence. It was inevitable that his moment of defeat would arrive. Hawker knew that one day he would meet up with someone who feared less than he or who cared about less than he, and he would take the final long step, sent by a bullet or knife blade or bomb or club into the last darkness.

Until death came knocking, though, he would live his life as fully as possible.

At the moment, that meant getting ready for the trip to Aspen. It meant packing carefully and effectively, preparing for any emergency. It meant getting ready to travel fast and light and to act surely, ruthlessly, without qualm or regret.

Hawker went for a short run through the streets of Denver,

then did a half-hour of tough calisthenics. Then he set about packing. He packed a leather flight bag with his personal clothing and needs. He could live out of the bag indefinitely, for months if need be.

Then he opened the two wooden boxes and began to carefully select the weaponry he might need while in the mountains. He spent more than an hour preparing, getting everything just right. As he did, he tried to imagine every eventuality and allow for it. To the vigilante, preparation was one of the most important aspects of any assignment. Furthermore, it was one of the most important aspects of any trip.

Hawker couldn't abide traveling with people who packed too much, who carried too much weight, who lived carelessly while on the road.

In the vigilante's mind, traveling was a craft. Traveling efficiently was something he took pride in. It increased the enjoyment of all his trips while lessening the hassle. Very, very few people, he had learned, traveled well.

When he was finished packing, he showered, shaved, then dressed himself in glove-soft woolen slacks, a silky chamois shirt, pure cotton socks, and Vibram-soled boots.

That done, he called Lomela to see if Tom Dulles had arrived at her cabin hideout yet. There was no answer. Where the hell could they be? The vigilante thought about the possibilities as he dialed SkyCab and arranged for a chopper ride over the mountains to Aspen. The woman on the phone seemed offended that he wanted a helicopter. They had several seats available on their private planes that afternoon, and if it was good enough for the likes of John Denver and Jimmy Buffett, then why not—

Hawker cut her off short and told her that price was no object. He wanted a chopper, and he wanted a pilot who had some time on his hands—preferably a Nam vet who had spent some time in-country.

The woman said she would try, though she clearly was not pleased to be forced out of her routine and now would actually have to use her brains to satisfy the needs of a customer.

The vigilante hung up, grumpy with the American working woman, especially the service secretary. He wondered why so many of them were bitchy, lazy, indifferent, self-important, and so generally worthless. Maybe it was because their National Organization of Women meetings kept them up late at night. Maybe it was because they all had embraced the symptoms of pre-menstrual syndrome as the proper behavior for the modern woman. Whatever the reason, they were irritating as hell. Hawker knew that out of all the hundreds of thousands of service secretaries around the country, there were undoubtedly some good ones—probably a dozen, maybe even more.

Hawker dialed Mountain Car Rental and got a bored but fairly efficient woman. She reserved a four-wheel-drive vehicle for him in Aspen. No, she couldn't tell him for sure if it would be a Bronco, a Cherokee, or a Blazer. Yes, he could pay cash if he left a sizable deposit. Yes, she would see that the vehicle was left for him at the airport.

The vigilante tried Lomela's number once more. No answer. He lifted his two duffels and stopped at the front desk.

He paid the deskman cash in advance for two weeks' room rental. He palmed a hundred-dollar bill and left just the corner showing when he asked the clerk to make sure no one was allowed access to his room while he was away.

The hundred disappeared into the clerk's pocket in a blur as the man made grave promises about the sacred rights of the hotel's guests.

Hawker got a cab to the airport and found his chopper and pilot waiting. The pilot was a twenty-three-year-old roustabout who would have looked more at home on a horse. Once they were off the ground and Denver was fading into a mass of geometries beneath them, Hawker fanned a pair of hundred-dollar bills and told the pilot he wanted a few detours on their way to Aspen.

The pilot removed his earphones. "You a drug runner?" he yelled over the whirring racket of the helicopter.

"Nope. A tourist."

"Bullshit. If you're a tourist, I'm Sylvester Stallone. You a cop?"

"Nope. I just want to do a little sightseeing."

"You look like a cop to me."

Hawker met the man's inquisitive look with a chuckle. "What are you, some kind of game-show host? I didn't hire this chopper to be asked questions. And I didn't pull these bills out of my pocket to liven up the conversation. Are you going to fly me around so I can do some sightseeing or not?"

"Don't get mad, mister. I just don't want to do anything illegal."

"Yeah? Are you sure you're not just afraid to fly something different than this hobbyhorse course to Aspen? Look, it's

117

nothing to be ashamed of, buddy. I hear it takes a pretty good chopper pilot to handle treetop stuff in these mountains. If you can't handle the thin air, just say so. Hell, I'm happy you've got the guts to admit it. I don't want to get splattered all over the side of a mountain."

The man's face flushed slightly. He reached out and took the bills. "Friend," he said, "if it had controls, I could fly an elephant up an ant's ass. There's no place in these hills I'm afraid to fly. Just tell me what you want to see, and I'll take you there. Like I said, as long as it's legal."

Trying not to smile, Hawker pulled out the map and showed the pilot. The pilot's name was Jake. Jake said the four abandoned silver mines shown on the chart were way the hell off the beaten track, but he could get to every one of them. No problem.

It had snowed in the mountains, and they flew over a fairy-tale world of silver trees sprinkled with silver snow, all glittering on a rolling blanket of white. Leadville was a gingerbread village between snowy peaks. Cars on Highway 24 were colorful toys on the twisty-turny mountain road, and the shadow of the helicopter blew past them like a dark cloud.

"We don't have far to go to that first mine. It's about ten klicks beyond that next peak." Jake nodded ahead to a towering mountain cap covered with white and veined with jagged rocks. It seemed to Hawker very unlikely that the chopper would ever make it up and over. "That's Mount Holy Cross. More than fourteen thousand feet high. A real monster, huh?"

"Are we going to try to get over it?" the vigilante asked, his voice calm.

"Naw, no way. I did it once, but it was real hairy. Too high, man. The blades got nothing to dig into. We need to cut west a bit anyway, so we'll sneak around it. What do you expect to see at these abandoned mine sites, anyway?"

"I don't expect to see anything," Hawker replied. "But I want to take a look just in case."

"I got it," the pilot said, snapping his fingers. "You're an investor, right? You got some kind of group maybe thinking of starting a new ski resort. You're thinking of maybe building something between Vail and Aspen, right?"

Hawker tried to look troubled. "Even if I did represent such a group, I couldn't tell you," he said. "Do you understand me, Jake? I've paid you well to fly me around, and I expect some professional discretion, okay? If our competition found out, they could undercut us or get some of those environmental hotheads out on the warpath. Hell, they kept the Olympic Games out of Colorado. We sure as hell wouldn't stand much of a chance if the wrong people found out."

"No problem." The man laughed. "Hell, I'm all for it. I can maybe keep my eye open for your group and make a small investment on the ground floor. Shit, I thought maybe one of those two duffels you loaded on board was maybe filled with cocaine. I was afraid you were going to ask me to drop it. I don't need to get involved in some big drug bust."

"No need to worry about that," the vigilante said, laughing. "I swear to you, there are no drugs in my duffel."

They came off the side of the mountain into a long valley. The valley was a cradle of open fields, sparse trees, and a raging river. The western edge was streaked with twisting brown ruts that disappeared into heavy woods. They were the tracks of vehicles.

"Why would there be cars up here?" the vigilante asked.

The pilot shook his head. "You got me. There's some kind of private hunting lodge up here, but it ain't hunting season. Maybe there's a group of bird watchers up here or something."

"Who owns the hunting lodge?"

"How the hell should I know? Rich people. Who else? These mountains are owned by people from all over the world. Arabs, Jews, Japs, maybe even a few Americans—actors and rock stars, mostly. They're the only ones who can afford it. Hell, a rich person doesn't figure he's made it till he can brag at cocktail parties about his condo in Aspen."

"How long has the lodge been here?"

"Longer than I've been here, friend. See it down there through the trees? It's that big log cabin place. The one right on the river."

The lodge was dimly visible beneath the trees, a great dark L-shape with a stone fireplace. The tire tracks all led directly to it, though there were no cars visible.

"What's that?" asked the vigilante. "See it hanging from the trees there?"

"Yeah. And it looks like the snow's all red beneath it. Like blood or something. What the hell? Hang on. I'm taking her down for a closer look."

The helicopter banked sharply as the pilot drove the craft downward within a couple of hundred feet of the ground. "They've got some deer hanging up there," Hawker said, relieved. He had been afraid he had stumbled onto the bodies of Dulles and Lomela. "They've got five or six of them, waiting to be butchered."

The pilot swore softly. "That's what I hate about these rich bastards," he said. "They buy property up here, and they think they own the goddamned mountains. Hell, it ain't even deer season, but they've gone ahead and shot more than they can probably use. Hell, see there? Half of them are does. The bastards! I'm gonna go in close and give them jerks a scare. Maybe they'll think we're game wardens."

Hawker shook his head. "I'm no fan of poachers, but I'm not up here looking for game law offenders. Skip the kamikaze act. Find me those silver mines."

"You're paying for the flight, Mr. Hawker," said the pilot stubbornly, "but I'm still at the controls. I'm going to give those bastards a little something to worry about, and then I'm gonna notify the state game warden when we get to Aspen. People like that need to be shown that the laws apply to them just like they do to everyone else."

The vigilante said nothing as the young pilot brought the craft hovering low over the trees in which hung the dead deer. Snow swirled away in a fog beneath them, and Hawker wasn't surprised to see several men come running out of the lodge.

But he was surprised to see that one of them carried something long and tubular over his shoulder.

Hawker grabbed the pilot's shoulder. "Get the hell out of here!" he yelled. "Now!"

Jake's eyes had grown wide. "What in the hell is that thing? He's—he's aiming it at us!"

121

"Damn it, get this chopper moving! It's some kind of ground-to-air weapon. He's going to drop us."

The pilot yanked the stick abruptly backward, and the helicopter jumped over the approaching trees with a burst of speed that sent Hawker's stomach up into his throat. He turned in his seat and looked behind them. *"Shit,"* he whispered grimly. Vectoring after them, fluttering with a tail of black smoke, was some kind of small rocket.

"Put her down," the vigilante said coolly. "Get her down below the treeline, or we're both dead."

The young pilot didn't have to be told twice. He shoved the stick forward, and they were immediately hurtling toward the ground, the branches of trees swarming past, going much too fast. Hawker was about to yell out, to offer more directions to the terrified pilot, when there was a deafening explosion, a burst of bright white light, and then the chopper was spinning wildly, dropping down through the trees, toward the mountain, and toward death.

THIRTEEN

There was a terrible slapping-cracking noise as breaking tree limbs slowed the twirling descent of the chopper. Then there was a bone-jarring crash much harder than what Hawker was prepared for.

"Fire!"

The scream of the young pilot yanked the vigilante from the gauzy twilight world of near-unconsciousness. The entire back section of the helicopter was ablaze with withering white flames. Hawker found his seat-belt clasp, reached behind for his duffel, then threw himself out the door onto the fresh snow.

"Help me! I can't move!"

The shriek was more like that of a terrified woman. But it wasn't a woman. It was the pilot. For some reason he couldn't get out of the blazing chopper.

The vigilante leaped to his feet—and immediately fell. His left ankle felt as if it had been jammed up into his leg. On his hands and knees he crawled toward the portside door of the aircraft. Jake was pounding frantically against the window, trying to get out.

"Don't let me burn, for God's sake!"

The vigilante locked his hands on the door latch—and heard his flesh sizzle. He yanked off his down vest, wrapped it around the handle, and tried again. Hawker put all his strength into it, all his weight, and finally the door snapped open.

The snow was deliciously cold as he tumbled backward onto the soft forest floor.

"My legs won't move. You got to pull me out, Mr. Hawker! Hurry. I can't—stand—this heat!"

The vigilante was by the man's side in an instant. He used one hand to try to shield his own face from the flames and the other on the release clasp of the seat belt. After long agonizing seconds, the belt finally broke free. Hawker grabbed Jake by the shirt and pulled him clear of the blazing chopper, dragging him onto the ground like a heavy sack.

For the first time, Hawker looked back toward the hunting lodge. The men who had shot them would be coming soon. People didn't use hand-carried ground-to-air missiles unless they planned to follow up and hide their own tracks. In this case, following up meant finishing the kill, hiding the bodies, and destroying all evidence of the chopper.

Who the hell were they, anyway? Left-wing reactionaries on a secret training mission? Drug-crazed hunters who would stop at nothing to keep from getting caught with their illegal kill? Or maybe the pilot had inadvertently stumbled onto Nek's secret hideout.

Whoever they were, the vigilante knew he didn't have much time to get ready for them.

"Jake? Can you hear me? Can you understand what I'm saying?" The vigilante held the pilot's head in his lap, trying to get some idea of how badly hurt he was. He didn't look good. There was absolutely no body movement below his waist. Apparently he had broken his spine in the crash. His face was ruby-red, the skin blistered like a barbecued frankfurter. His hands were a blackened mess. "I'm going to try to put you over my shoulder and carry you out of here," Hawker said.

"No!" The young pilot's eyes fluttered open. "Too—tired. Let me stay . . . Snow feels so good, so . . . cool . . ." Hawker felt the man's muscles contract violently as his green eyes turned suddenly foggy. "A missile," the pilot whispered in fading disbelief. "They hit us . . . with . . . a damn *missile.*"

Then his mouth dropped open as his body became a solid meaty weight in the vigilante's arms.

He was dead.

Disgusted, Hawker spat into the clean snow—and realized for the first time that he was bleeding from the mouth. He touched his face and saw more blood on his fingers. The windshield of the chopper had apparently burst and cut him. He must have looked like one hell of a mess.

But at least he was alive. And fairly mobile. That's more than he could say for Jake.

He hadn't known the pilot well, but he had seemed like a nice kid, a square shooter who wasn't afraid to put the cards on the table. It was a rare quality these days. Hawker rolled the body over and patted the kid's back pocket, took out the billfold, and slipped it into his own pants before he put on his down vest. The pilot wore no wedding ring, but there would be a girl somewhere, and her picture and probably her phone number would be in the wallet. Hawker would call her when he got the chance.

Suddenly, there was the distant crashing noise of men rushing through the woods. And there were voices: "This way. It went down someplace over here!"

The vigilante could hear voices coming nearer. What was it that seemed familiar about the voices? Then he realized: several of the men had heavy German accents.

That's when he knew. That's when he knew that, if he had been in danger before, the danger was now tripled.

This was Bill Nek's hunting lodge. And these were Bill Nek's men coming to get him.

Hawker got painfully to his feet, drew a can-shaped Ingram MAC10 submachine gun from the heavy duffel, and hobbled off through the forest cursing the fresh sheet of snow that covered the ground. It was impossible to travel without leaving tracks! He tried moving from one bare rock to another, but they were too far apart and it didn't really work anyway. Nek's men would find his tracks and be on him in a matter of minutes.

What the hell was he going to do?

He had no choice. He had to run as best he could on the bad ankle and hope the Germans wasted enough time at the crash site for him to get away. He knew how unlikely that was, but he had to hope.

Ahead the forest opened into rocky crags without a horizon. Could the river be ahead? Hawker wished he had paid more attention to the lay of the land. Maybe he'd luck out and find a cave.

There was a thud in the snowbank ahead of him, followed by the Winchester whistle-whack of a rifle being fired. Hawker turned to see three men come charging out of the woods after him. All of them carried rifles. And now they were all firing at him.

Hawker checked the safety tang of the Ingram to make sure it was on full automatic, and he turned and fired, holding the weapon in one hand at hip level. The little Ingram had an effective range of only seventy-five meters, but it could spray three hundred rounds of 9mm slugs in fifteen seconds.

The vigilante waved the weapon back and forth only once, and the thirty-two-round clip was empty—and the three men lay kicking and writhing in splotches of bright scarlet on the hillside, as the clatter of the submachine gun echoed through the mountains.

Hawker threw the empty clip back into the duffel and slid in a fresh clip before hobbling over the hill. There was a snowy embankment ahead. He hoped like hell there was a cave or something on the other side. He stopped for a moment and looked back before climbing over the embankment—and wished immediately that he had not bothered.

A man was kneeling on the hillside beneath the trees, holding something dark and tubular on his shoulder. The vigilante knew immediately that it must be a weapon similar to that which had knocked the helicopter from the sky. An army M72 disposable missile launcher, maybe.

Whatever the hell it was, Hawker didn't want to be around when it went off.

He took three long steps toward the embankment, wincing with pain, aware of a weird whooshing noise and a piercing whine as he rolled over the edge of the snow mound expecting to see a hill—but there was no hill, just a sheer, sheer drop—then he was falling, tumbling, smacking, rolling through powdered snow, and a moment later there was an explosion and the whole top lifted off the embankment and rolled toward him.

FOURTEEN

James Hawker was aware of darkness and of numbing cold. He could hear voices, too. Strangely muted voices, as if they were coming through a wall.

He strained to open his eyes until he realized his eyes were already open. An opaque light was noticeable directly in front of him, like light beams through crystal. With a start, he realized that he must be buried under snow. The voices he heard must be the voices of Bill Nek's men looking for him.

The vigilante took quick inventory of his body. He could move his toes, his legs, his arms, his head. He took a deep breath of genuine relief. He might suffocate, but at least he wasn't paralyzed.

He seemed to be in some kind of natural culvert of rock, covered with snow. Because of the culvert, he had a little room to move in, and there was obviously also enough air trapped for him to breathe.

Falling into the culvert had no doubt saved him. Now it might even provide a way for him to escape.

But Hawker didn't move. The voices seemed very close, although he could not understand what they were saying. It was possible that the men were walking over him at that very moment. Hawker waited motionlessly just as long as he could stand the cold.

It was probably ten or fifteen minutes. It seemed like two hours. He realized that he would have to get his body moving soon if he were not to suffer severe frostbite. It had been some time since he had heard the last of the voices. He edged himself over onto his stomach. Snow and gravel rained down on his head. Hawker paused for a long moment, fearful that this might be the beginning of another avalanche. When all was still once more, he began to move again.

There seemed to be some kind of opening ahead. He began to burrow his way along, pushing the duffel bag ahead of him. To the vigilante's delight, the culvert widened unexpectedly. The roof was no longer of snow—it was made of rock. He was at the mouth of some kind of shallow cave. Now, instead of being unbearably cold, the snow and the rock seemed to work together to produce a warm stillness. Hawker found a ledge, and he sat with his head almost brushing the roof of the cave. He blew on his numb fingers and flexed his toes, warming himself. Yes, he could make it here for a while. He could survive here until it was safe to leave.

The vigilante checked his watch: 2:14 P.M. The sun would set behind the mountains in another three hours.

Hawker unzipped the duffel and searched through the firearms and heavy ordnance until he found his good black wool sweater and his black watch cap. He put them both on for extra warmth, then used the duffel for a pillow and settled back.

For a long time he had been refining his ability to use his mind to control his mind *and* his body. Hawker called upon that ability now. He ordered his body to relax as he switched his mind to a numb but still alert state of hypnosis. In a back compartment of his mind he was aware of his heartbeat getting slower and slower as his body temperature stabilized. He could almost feel his nerves and body healing in this deep meditative state.

James Hawker told his mind to reawaken at sunset, and then he followed hypnosis into sleep.

He awoke in darkness, aware of pain.

James Hawker flexed his neck, his arms, his legs, his swollen ankle. The helicopter crash had hurt him more than he had suspected. He wished he could go back to sleep and not wake up for a long, long time. But in this land of ice and silent mountains, he knew such a sleep might mean death.

The vigilante sat and touched the top of the narrow cave. When he felt able, he rifled through the duffel bag until he found the little Tekna waterproof light. He twisted the cap and shined the beam around. It made an eerie light, like looking up from the inside of a grave. Then he began to slide toward the mouth of the cave. Soon the rock ceiling disappeared and the roof was formed by only ice and snow. What had happened to Nek's men? Hawker wondered. Was there any chance they would have left a guard to watch for him? No, that was unlikely. Completely covered by snow, they would have assumed that he was either dying or dead.

Furthermore, it was after sunset—at least, it seemed so in this dark world.

Hawker removed the cannonlike .44 magnum Smith & Wesson revolver from the duffel. He checked to make sure it was not loaded, then he used the butt to chip away at the overhead ice. When he had almost knocked a hole through the ceiling, the whole thing suddenly collapsed on him, and for one terrifying moment he thought he really might be buried alive. But then he poked his head through to see a silver cusp of moon and bright Venus glowing over the bronze afterglow of sunset.

The vigilante pulled his weapons up behind him and set off hobbling in the direction of the hunting lodge.

What were the chances of finding Jimmy Estes and Chuck Phillips? Hawker had no idea. But injured or not, he was damned determined to take a close look at the hunting lodge.

He moved along slowly through the woods, aware that there might be guards waiting for him anywhere. As he walked, he loaded the .44 magnum revolver. The big cartridges felt like minitorpedoes in his cold hands. He slid a fresh clip into the Ingram and pulled out the wire stock so that he could belt the submachine gun over his shoulder. Into a nylon waist pack he put several types of grenades and plastic explosives. Whatever Nek had waiting for him, he was determined to be ready.

As Hawker walked, his ankle began to loosen. He began to feel better. The adrenaline rush he always felt before the beginning of a firefight began to move through him. Nek and his men had numbers on their side, but he had surprise on his. More important, though, he had experience.

Ahead, he could now see the uniform darkness of the log hunting lodge. There were lights on, and the windows were square yellow eyes. He could also see the dim vertical shapes of the dead deer hanging on the rack. Hawker swore beneath his breath. If it hadn't been for spotting the deer, the young pilot would be alive now.

The vigilante moved deliberately from tree to tree, staying in the shadows. He wanted to hide the canvas duffel filled with the rest of his ordnance someplace where he could find it quickly. He noticed a tent-shaped wooden hogs' shed near the venison rack. He approached it from the side, then poked his head in. It was too dark to see anything, so he chanced flicking on the little flashlight.

The vigilante almost screamed in shock.

Only a few inches from his nose were the pale face and the wide dark eyes of Lieutenant Tom Dulles staring at him. They had thrown him into the shed so that his back had lodged on a stack of tinder wood, giving him an odd look of impermanence, as if he were frozen on film in the midst of a bad fall. He wore the same beige down vest Hawker had seen him wear before, but now it was stained black with blood. The blood had dripped down and caked on the face of the corpse resting beneath him, the corpse of the lovely Lomela Carthay; Lomela of the full warm breasts and the wanting lips and the motherly touch and the thrusting, fertile hips. In the center of her forehead was a dark hole, and her face looked oddly swollen, misshapen.

The vigilante knew that a bullet through the head could do that and worse to a human face.

Lying on the ground next to Lomela was the body of the young pilot.

Hawker switched off the light and sat down quickly in the snow, making an uncontrollable growling noise.

Bastards!

He had stumbled onto Nek's body locker. It was almost full—and all in only a day. Tom Dulles and Lomela had come up into the mountains looking for old Robert Charles Carthay, who had sworn to bring Nek to justice himself. And they had paid dearly for their concern.

What had happened to old man Carthay? Hawker hoped like hell that Lomela hadn't brought her two kids with her.

No, she would have never done that. She cared too much for them.

The vigilante squeezed his hands into heavy fists. He had liked Dulles as much as he had liked any man. And he had been Lomela's lover. He had known her in private hours, and he had seen what a tender creature she was with her now-orphaned children. Tom and Lomela had been two bright lives, two vital people. Now Nek had killed them and thrown them into a hogs' shed beside the venison rack like so much butchered meat.

James Hawker got up slowly. It had been a long time since he had felt what he was now feeling. He was feeling anger, cold and deadly anger, like bile coursing through his body.

And only one thing would satisfy that anger—revenge. Harsh and bloody revenge.

And bloody revenge, Hawker decided, was exactly what he would now take—a revenge as brutal and demanding as the life of Bill Nek.

If Nek wasn't here, Hawker would track him as long as need be, and he would kill the old bastard with his bare hands.

The vigilante unstrapped the Ingram and drew the .44 magnum. Carrying the submachine gun in his left hand and the huge revolver in his right, Hawker began to move slowly toward the house.

FIFTEEN

The dark figure appeared from the trees so quickly and hit him so hard that Hawker didn't have time to react. He was instantly on the ground fighting for his life as a big man tried to kill him.

The man had something in his hand, something heavy and hard and silver—a knife.

Hawker dropped the MAC10 submachine gun and caught the man's hand as he brought the knife slashing toward his face. The vigilante used the man's momentum to send him rolling over his head. Hawker was on his feet in an instant, and he used the .44 magnum like a club. The butt of the revolver made a sickening plastic-smack sound against the man's face. His entire jaw swung apart from his cheek, his whole face crushed. He toppled to the ground with a groan.

Hawker gave him an insurance kick to the throat, and the attacker lay soundlessly. The vigilante snapped the .44 into its chest holster, hunched over the body, and picked up the knife.

He recognized the size and feel of the weapon instantly. It

was his Randall survival knife, the one taken from him back in Denver. He searched the body of the man and found the custom scabbard strapped to his belt. He stripped it away from the man's hips, quickly threaded his own belt through, and buckled it tight. It felt good to have the solid weight of the Randall on his hip once again.

Hawker picked up the MAC10, cleaned the butt of the Smith & Wesson in the snow, and moved on. Behind the house the vigilante could now decipher the dim outline of some kind of cottage. A single window glowed through the trees. In the pale mountain night, Hawker could also now see the shape of two men standing in front of the cottage. Guards? Probably. But what were they guarding? Hawker could only hope that the three old miners were inside.

He decided to have a look. Sliding from tree to tree in the darkness, he moved to the backside of the huge lodge. The new snow crunched beneath his feet. Owls called back and forth in the distance. The wind made an exotic rattling sound in the aspen trees, like oriental wind chimes. It was one of those beautiful Rocky Mountain nights, a night of rarefied air, of high laser-bright stars, of wine and cheese parties in Denver, of pre-ski parties in expensive Aspen. It was the kind of Colorado night that people sang about and the whole world fantasized about. For the vigilante, though, it was a night for hunting, a night for collecting old debts. For him, it was a Colorado night built for killing. The pale moon gave some light, but not too much. The wind made enough noise to cover his footfall, but not so much noise that he could not hear.

Hawker was still surprised that Nek didn't have more

guards out. But then, why should he? Dulles was dead. Lomela was dead. The three old miners were once again prisoners. And presumably Hawker was frozen under several feet of snow.

Why should Bill Nek be worried? His enemies were all eliminated, and he would soon own the Chiquita Silver Mine—or so he thought.

His face a grim mask, cold and unemotional, Hawker stopped a few dozen yards from the side of the cottage and slung the MAC10 over his shoulder. He leaned into a tree, letting his black sweater and wool watch cap make him a part of the shadows. The two guards stood at the front of the cottage, their feet shifting uncomfortably in the cold. One of them was smoking a cigarette. His rifle rested against the side of the little house. The other held his rifle in the crook of his arm.

Hawker didn't hesitate. He strode boldly toward the front door of the cabin. The guards jumped to attention, fearing an attack. "Hey," said the vigilante easily. "How are you guys tonight?"

They both visibly relaxed. "Not so bad," said one of them in a light German accent. "A little cold, but not too bad. Been worse."

"You got business out here?" said the other guard, a little suspiciously. "I don't remember seeing you—"

He never got a chance to finish the sentence. As the guard stuck the cigarette in his mouth and leaned toward his rifle, the vigilante brought the brass butt of the Randall knife down on his head, then threw himself headlong into the belly of the second guard, who was already leveling his rifle to shoot.

Hawker tried to wrestle the rifle from his hands, but the guard kicked up hard with his knee, catching Hawker just to the right of the scrotum. It sent a pain shock flashing through his guts, and beads of sweat formed on his head. But he still did not go down to the ground.

The guard managed to yank the rifle free, and he used it like a baseball bat to swing at the vigilante's head. Hawker ducked under the rifle and drove the brutal blade of the Randall attack knife up under the ribs of the guard. The 7-1/2-inch blade found the man's heart. As the guard opened his mouth to scream, a large bloody bubble formed on his lips. It popped in silence as Hawker pulled the knife free.

The guard fell dead to the ground.

The vigilante limped to the door of the cottage. It was padlocked. Cursing softly, he returned to the first fallen guard and took the keys from the dead man's pocket. The lock was cold against his fingers, but it finally snapped open. Hawker swung open the door.

Inside, the lights were on. Three old men sat at a table by a wood stove playing cards. They looked up in surprise at the vigilante.

"Holy dogshit," said Robert Carthay, a wide-shouldered, balding man with suspenders, "if it ain't Mr. James Hawker. Hey, boys, this here's the man I was telling you 'bout."

All three men dropped their cards onto the table as they stood to greet the vigilante. But Hawker was in no mood for social niceties. And they had no time. "Look," he said quickly, "can you three find your way back down the mountain? Can you make it on your own?"

Carthay looked offended. "Listen here, you young buck. We spent more time walking these hills than you've spent toyin' with your pecker. We can find our way out in a coal-dust storm at night in the rain when it's foggy. Shit, I guess. Ain't that right, boys?"

"Damn tootin', Bobby."

"You tell the young fart, Bob-O!"

Hawker motioned to them to keep their voices down. "Then grab your coats and get going. And I mean now. There's going to be some real ugly stuff going on here in about five minutes."

"We're gonna stay right here and help," Carthay said stubbornly. "I ain't gonna be happy till I get my hands around the throat of that son of a bitch Bill Nek. Why, I'm going to pull his ears off—"

"Nek's inside?"

"You goddamn right he is! I heard the old bastard yell at somebody not more than an hour ago. It ain't gonna be the last time he yells tonight, either. I'm gonna make that turd beg for his life, after the way he's treated us!"

"Sure, you do that," Hawker said sharply. "Do that, and you'll get involved in what's going to happen tonight. Give you plenty to tell the cops, won't it? And they'll give you plenty more to tell the judges in Denver. You'll spend all the money you make from the Chiquita Silver Mine on lawyers, and all three of you will probably go to jail." Hawker shook his finger at them. "You three had a chance to make some money a long time ago, but you let Nek screw it up for you. Are you going to let him screw you up again? Don't be dumb shits. Get the hell out of here while you can. Keep yourselves in the clear." Hawker looked at old Robert Carthay pointedly. "You've got grandchildren to think about, Mr. Carthay. Are you going to risk their future, too?"

The old man rubbed his grizzled chin, thinking. "I wouldn't want to hurt Lomela or them kids," he said softly. "They 'bout the only things I care about in this here world."

Hawker cringed, thinking how badly Carthay was going to take the news of his daughter's murder. But he couldn't be told now. He'd never agree to leave the mountain. Nor would his two friends. "Then get a move on," Hawker said. "Get the hell out of here, and don't turn back, no matter what you hear. Get your coats on. It's cold as hell out there. Take some of those blankets, and here's some money—"

"Listen to this young fart," said Jimmy Estes. "Sounds like a damned Jewish mother. Boy, we was hiking these hills long before you pissed your first diaper."

"Yeah," Chuck Phillips put in quickly, "but we'll still take some money. Guards took all ours, and we may need it. Thanks, Mister Hawker. Thanks for talking some sense into this old fool beside me."

The vigilante handed a wad of bills to Phillips, then hurried the three of them out the door and into the woods. He watched them until they disappeared into the darkness, three resolute shapes against the loom of the mountains that had been their homes for so long.

Once they had gone, Hawker sat on the door seal of the cabin, watching the hunting lodge. He sat quietly, letting his body rest, letting the aching ankle take a break from the work he knew it must soon do, letting his mind vector this way and that, seeking a plan. But in truth, he wanted no plan. He knew exactly what he was going to do. Tom Dulles wouldn't have approved. Dulles was a lawman in the best sense of the word. Lomela wouldn't have approved either, though she would probably understand.

But in some strange way, Hawker knew it was what he must do. Nek was an old man. He would undoubtedly die a natural death before long.

But the vigilante knew he could not allow that to happen. The life of William Nek was too fouled by his own deeds to be allowed such a clean exit from life.

No, Dulles wouldn't have approved, and Lomela wouldn't have approved. But they were now cold corpses, thrown into a hogs' shed to be buried later.

They no longer had any say.

Hawker was a master of revenge. And he knew the decision was now all his.

SIXTEEN

When Carthay and the others had a half-hour head start down the mountain, Hawker stood and checked the Ingram to make sure that it was fully loaded and that he had plenty of extra clips. He took the .44 magnum revolver from the holster strapped across his chest, spun the cylinder in the light of the cabin, then slid it easily back into the holster.

In his free right hand, he took two Army TH3 incendiary hand grenades, pulled the pin on each with his teeth, and, still holding the safety spoons in place, walked calmly to the front door and knocked.

He could hear men's voices inside, could hear music. The door swung open wide, and Hawker got a momentary glimpse of one of the Germans he recognized from Nek's Denver estate.

"Special delivery," the vigilante said sweetly, tossing both grenades into the huge front room of the lodge. In reply to the German's sudden look of terror and confusion, Hawker added, "Don't worry—you don't have to sign." Then he jumped from the steps, sprint-hobbled toward some trees, and dove behind them as a huge explosion shook the earth.

He turned to see the entire interior front section of the lodge engulfed in gaseous white flames. The heat was withering. Hawker wasn't surprised, nor was he shocked to hear the terrible screams coming from inside. The incendiary grenades were filled with thermate, a lethal chemical developed by the Chemical Warfare Service of the United States. Each thermate grenade would burn for nearly a minute at more than two thousand degrees, setting everything within twenty yards immediately in flames.

William Nek's hunting lodge was now burning as if it were made from Georgia lighter pine.

The vigilante drew the big Smith & Wesson revolver and waited. In a few moments, the front door flew open and men began to sprint out like ants from a damaged anthill. They all seemed to have weapons, and they fired wildly into the night, more concerned with escaping the terrible heat than with killing their attacker.

As they exited, the vigilante aimed and fired carefully. One by one, the .44 magnum blew the first six men backward, knocking two of them right out of their shoes.

Hawker wasn't surprised when the door was suddenly thrown closed. Someone had decided it was safer to face the fire than to face the lone man outside.

Quickly, Hawker lumbered to the side of the house, smashed out a window, and tossed in another thermate grenade. He used his last three incendiary grenades at the back of the house. Four times he opened fire on men as they tried to flee out the back door or windows. Four times men died. The vigilante worked his way to the side of the great house, the only section that now was not in flames. He could see men peeking out the door. When he stepped into view, the men opened fire, and Hawker had to dive toward cover.

Slugs kicked up a line of snow and dirt behind him as he rolled into a ditch.

"Nek! Bill Nek! I want you!" Hawker's cold voice echoed through the night.

More shots rang out, vectoring on the position of his voice. The vigilante turned the Ingram on full automatic and sprayed the side door and windows of the lodge. Inside, a man screamed. Another came crashing through the window, clawing at his bloody face.

"Nek! Get your ass out here, old man!"

The vigilante was standing now, his blazing gray eyes and square chin illuminated by the raging fire that now consumed the lodge.

On the second floor, a window shattered and a man opened fire with a wide-bore shotgun. Snow plumed around Hawker as he immediately held the freshly loaded submachine gun on full fire. A man wearing only underwear came floundering through the jagged glass, shotgun in hand. He landed heavily, kicked wildly for a moment, then lay still.

"If you don't come out now, old man, I'm going to let you burn to death!" Hawker was standing at the corner of the house so that he could see both the front and side exits. How many of the Silver King's men had he killed? At least fifteen. Maybe more with the grenades. Nek couldn't have many more bodyguards left inside. And he sure as hell didn't have much more time. The hunting lodge was a crackling, steaming box of flames now. It crossed the vigilante's mind that Nek might already be dead: burned to death or killed by the percussion of the heavy ordnance.

But then, at the side door, he saw the evil old face, the contorted expression of anger and desperation, the man who had worked hard to ruin the lives of his three partners, the man who had destroyed many men on his climb to the top, the man who had murdered his two friends Tom Dulles and Lomela Carthay, the man he now wanted to kill as badly as he had ever wanted to kill anyone.

Bill Nek came through the door slowly, his eyes wide and glazed with an expression of insane desperation. In his right hand was a revolver. And the barrel of the revolver was jammed into the ear of the blond and beautiful Melissa Nek. "I'll kill her, Hawker. I swear to God I'll kill her if you don't let me pass!"

The vigilante stood his ground, the .44 magnum in his right hand pointed at the ground. "Why should I care if you kill your wife, Nek? She doesn't mean anything to me."

"Bullshit! You've been sleeping with her, Hawker! She's in love with you. Told me so herself. Now put down that side-arm, and I'll let her live. And I'll let you live, too, though I should have your damned nuts cut off for fucking with something that's mine."

He had the woman's arm twisted up behind her back, and the woman's face was contorted with pain as she said, "Don't listen to him, James! He's lying! He'll kill you the moment you put down your gun. He'll kill me, too."

146

The vigilante paid no attention to the pleas of the woman. His eyes were still focused on Bill Nek, the Silver King. "Okay, Nek," he said slowly. "I'll let you pass. I'll put down the gun. But first you have to tell me something. Tell me who killed Dulles and the woman. Was it you?"

The old man was less than thirty feet from the vigilante now, trying to slide past him sideways as he replied, "Who killed them? I killed them, that's who. They come up here snooping into things that was none of their business, trying to get involved in my affairs. They had no right. None at all. You goddamn right I killed them. I'm going to kill those three old fools I got locked up out back, too—leastaways, the moment they sign the mine over to me, I am. People got no business messing in my affairs, Hawker. I got more money than them. That gives me more right, doesn't it? I tried to tell Dulles that. Tried to make him beg for his life. Wouldn't do it. Wouldn't admit that I'm the better man and I got the right."

"You tried to make Dulles beg?" Hawker said in a deadly calm voice.

"And then I shot him." The old man laughed, showing a row of very black teeth. "But that don't mean nothin' 'cause now you're going to put that gun down, and I'm going to leave you and sweet Melissa here—"

In that instant, the woman suddenly lunged to the side. The vigilante tilted the .44 magnum just over ninety degrees and fired before Nek could finish his sentence. The Smith & Wesson sounded like a cannon going off. Melissa and Bill Nek both dropped in their tracks.

The old man jolted backward, and his face was immediately transformed into a spongy horror of red gore. His hands clawed at the sky, and his legs kicked spasmodically.

The woman got shakily to her feet, staring at the gruesome figure that lay on the white snow. Bill Nek's eyes opened, straining to focus. Hawker stood over him now as the woman leaned against him as if to keep from fainting. The old man's eyes looked at Hawker, then at the woman, as he gasped, "You've killed me, daughter, you've killed me—" Then a gush of blood vomited from his mouth and his eyes froze in the wide exclamation of death.

Hawker looked incredulously at Melissa Nek. "That's the hold he had over you? You were his daughter and he married you?"

The woman pulled away from the vigilante and took a step toward the corpse of the Silver King. After a moment's hesitation, she turned and lifted her hand toward Hawker. "Take me away from here, James," she said in a tiny voice. "I owe you three hundred thousand dollars. That's all you need to know."

ABOUT THE AUTHOR

Randy Wayne White was born in Ashland, Ohio, in 1950. Best known for his series featuring retired NSA agent Doc Ford, he has published over twenty crime fiction and nonfiction adventure books. White began writing while working as a fishing guide in Florida, where most of his books are set. His earlier writings include the Hawker series, which he published under the pen name Carl Ramm. White has received several awards for his fiction, and his novels have been featured on the *New York Times* bestseller list. He was a monthly columnist for *Outside* magazine and has contributed to several other publications, as well as lectured throughout the United States and travelled extensively. White currently lives on Pine Island in South Florida, and remains an active member of the community through his involvement with local civic affairs as well as the restaurant Doc Ford's Sanibel Rum Bar and Grill.

THE HAWKER SERIES

FROM OPEN ROAD MEDIA

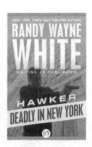

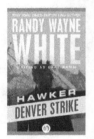

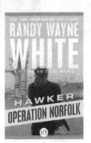

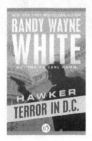

OPEN ROAD

INTEGRATED MEDIA

INTEGRATED MEDIA

Find a full list of our authors and
titles at www.openroadmedia.com

FOLLOW US
@OpenRoadMedia